PRAISE FOR
VISIONS OF SUGAR PLUMS

"May become a literary equivalent of *It's a Wonderful Life* . . . a warm, fuzzy wending despite the occasional explosion, smoldering plastic Santa, and rampaging elf."
—*Boston Globe*

"A top-notch read . . . a cure-all for the blues no matter what the season."
—*The Oakland Press*

"[A] special holiday treat."
—*The State* (Columbia, SC)

VISIONS OF SUGAR PLUMS

JANET EVANOVICH

St. Martin's Paperbacks

VISIONS OF SUGAR PLUMS

ISBN: 0-312-98634-3

Printed in the United States of America

St. Martin's Press hardcover edition / November 2002
St. Martin's Paperbacks edition / November 2003

St. Martin's Paperbacks are published by St. Martin's Press, 175 Fifth Avenue, New York, NY 10010.

10 9 8 7 6 5 4 3 2 1

This book was Plumtacularly edited and titled
by Jennifer Enderlin.
Yahoo, Jen!

ONE

My NAME IS Stephanie Plum and I've got a strange man in my kitchen. He appeared out of nowhere. One minute I was sipping coffee, mentally planning out my day. And then the next minute . . . *poof*, there he was.

He was over six feet, with wavy blond hair pulled into a ponytail, deep-set brown eyes, and an athlete's body. He looked to be late twenties, maybe thirty. He was dressed in jeans, boots, a grungy white thermal shirt hanging loose over the jeans, and a beat-up black leather jacket hanging on broad shoulders. He was sporting two days of beard growth, and he didn't look happy.

"Well, isn't this perfect," he said, clearly disgusted, hands on hips, taking me in.

My heart was tap-dancing in my chest. I was at a total loss. I didn't know what to think or what to say. I didn't know who he was or how he got into my kitchen. He was frightening, but even more than that he had me flustered. It was like going to a birthday party and arriving a day early. It was like . . . what the heck's going on?

"How?" I asked. "What?"

"Hey, don't ask me, lady," he said. "I'm as surprised as you are."

"How'd you get into my apartment?"

"Sweet cakes, you wouldn't believe me if I told you." He moved to the refrigerator, opened the door, and helped himself to a beer. He cracked the beer open, took a long pull, and wiped his mouth with the back of his hand. "You know how people get beamed down on *Star Trek*? It's sort of like that."

Okay, so I've got a big slob of a guy drinking beer in my kitchen, and I think he might be crazy. The only other possibility I can come up with is that I'm hallucinating and he isn't real. I smoked some pot in college but that was about it. Don't think I'd get a flashback from wacky tobacky. There were mushrooms on the pizza last night. Could that be it?

Fortunately, I work in bail bond enforcement, and I'm sort of used to scary guys showing up in closets and under beds. I inched my way across the kitchen, stuck my hand into my brown bear cookie jar, and pulled out my .38 five-shot Smith & Wesson.

"Cripes," he said, "what are you gonna do, shoot me? Like that would change anything." He looked more closely at the gun and shook his head in another wave of disgust. "Honey, there aren't any bullets in that gun."

"There might be one," I said. "I might have one chambered."

"Yeah, right." He finished the beer and sauntered out of the kitchen, into the living room. He looked around and moved to the bedroom.

"Hey," I yelled. "Where do you think you're going?"

He didn't stop.

"That's it," I told him. "I'm calling the police."

"Give me a break," he said. "I'm having a really shitty day." He kicked his boots off and flopped onto my bed, scoping out the room from his prone position. "Where's the television?"

"In the living room."

"Oh man, you don't even have a television in your bedroom. How crapola is this?"

I cautiously moved closer to the bed, and I reached out and touched him.

"Yeah, I'm real," he said. "Sort of. And all

my equipment works." He smiled for the first time. It was a knock-your-socks-off smile. Dazzling white teeth and good-humored eyes that crinkled at the corners. "In case you're interested."

The smile was good. The news was bad. I didn't know what *sort of real* meant. And I wasn't sure I liked the idea that his equipment worked. All in all, it didn't do a lot to help my heart rate. Truth is, I'm pretty much a chickenshit bounty hunter. Still, while I'm not the world's bravest person, I can bluff with the best of them, so I did an eye roll. "Get a grip."

"You'll come around," he said. "They always do."

"They?"

"Women. Women love me," he said.

Good thing I didn't have a bullet chambered as threatened because I'd definitely shoot this guy. "Do you have a name?"

"Diesel."

"Is that your first name or your last name?"

"That's my whole name. Who are *you*?"

"Stephanie Plum."

"You live here alone?"

"No."

"That's a big fib," he said. "You have *living alone* written all over you."

I narrowed my eyes. "Excuse me?"

"You're not exactly a sex goddess," he said. "Hair from hell. Baggy sweatpants. No makeup. Lousy personality. Not that there isn't some potential. You have an okay shape. What are you, 34B? And you've got a good mouth. Nice pouty lips." He threw me another smile. "A guy could get ideas looking at those lips."

Great. The nutcase who somehow got into my apartment was getting ideas about my lips. Thoughts of serial rapists and sex killings went racing through my mind. My mother's warnings echoed in my ears. *Watch out for strangers. Keep your door locked.* Yes, but it's not my fault, I reasoned. My door *was* locked. What's with that?

I took his boots, carried them to the front door, and threw them into the hall. "Your boots are in the hall," I yelled. "If you don't come get them, I'm pitching them down the trash chute."

My neighbor, Mr. Wolesky, stepped out of the elevator. He was holding a small white bakery bag in his hand. "Look at this," he said, "I'm starting the day with a doughnut. That's what Christmas does to me. It makes me crazy and then I need a doughnut. Four days to Christmas and the stores are picked clean," he said. "And they all say everything's on sale but I know they jack up the prices. They always gotta gouge you at Christmas. There should be a law. Somebody should look into it."

Mr. Wolesky unlocked his door, lurched inside, and slammed the door after himself. The door lock clicked into place, and I heard Mr. Wolesky's television go on.

Diesel elbowed me aside, went into the hall, and retrieved his boots. "You know, you have a real attitude problem," he said.

"Attitude this," I told him, closing my door, locking him out of the apartment.

The bolt shot back, the lock tumbled, and Diesel opened the door, walked to the couch, and sat down to put his boots on.

Hard to pick an emotion here. Confused and astounded would be high on the list. Scared bonkers wasn't far behind. "How'd you do that?" I said, squeaky-voiced and breathless. "How'd you unlock my door?"

"I don't know. It's just one of those things we can do."

Goosebumps prickled on my forearms. "Now I'm really creeped out."

"Relax. I'm not going to hurt you. Hell, I'm supposed to make your life better." He gave a snort and another bark of laughter at that. "Yeah, right," he said.

Deep breath, Stephanie. Not a terrific time to hyperventilate. If I passed out from lack of oxygen God knows what would happen. Suppose he was from outer space, and he conducted an anal probe while I was unconscious? A shiver ripped through me. Yuk! "What are we looking at here?" I asked him. "Ghost? Vampire? Space alien?"

He slouched back onto the couch and zapped the television on. "You're in the ballpark."

I was at à loss. How do you get rid of someone who can unlock locks? You can't even have him arrested by the police. And even if I decided to call the police, what would I say? I have a sort-of-real guy in my apartment?

"Suppose I cuffed you and chained you to something. What then?"

He was channel surfing, concentrating on the television. "I could get loose."

"Suppose I shot you?"

"I'd be pissed off. And it's not smart to piss me off."

"But could I kill you? Could I hurt you?"

"What is this, twenty questions? I'm looking for a game here. What time is it, anyway? And where am I?"

"You're in Trenton, New Jersey. It's eight o'clock in the morning. And you didn't answer my question."

He flipped the television off. "Crud. Trenton. I should have guessed. Eight in the morning. I have a whole day to look forward to. Wonderful. And the answer to your question is . . . a qualified no. It wouldn't be easy to kill me, but I suppose if you put your mind to it you could come up with something."

I went to the kitchen and phoned my next-door neighbor, Mrs. Karwatt. "I was wondering if you could come over for just a second," I said. "There's something I'd like to show you." A moment later, I ushered Mrs. Karwatt into my living room. "What do you see?" I asked her. "Is there anyone sitting on my couch?"

"There's a man on your couch," Mrs. Karwatt said. "He's big, and he has a blond ponytail. Is that the right answer?"

"Just checking," I said to Mrs. Karwatt. "Thanks."

Mrs. Karwatt left but Diesel remained.

"She could see you," I said to him.

"Well, duh."

He'd been in my apartment for almost a half hour now, and he hadn't done a full head rotation or tried to wrestle me down to the ground. That was a good sign, right? My mother's voice returned. *It means nothing. Don't let your guard down. He could be a maniac!* Problem was, the maniac thoughts were banging up against a gut feeling that he was an okay guy. Pushy and arrogant and generally obnoxious, but not criminally insane. Of course, it's possible my instincts were swayed by the fact that he was incredibly sexy-looking. And he smelled wonderful.

"What are you doing here?" I asked him, curiosity beginning to override panic.

He stood and stretched and scratched his stomach. "How about if I'm the friggin' Spirit of Christmas."

My mouth dropped open. The friggin' Spirit of Christmas. I must be dreaming. Probably I dreamed I called Mrs. Karwatt, too. The friggin' Spirit of Christmas. That's actually pretty funny. "Here's the thing," I said to him. "I have enough Christmas spirit. I don't need you."

"Not my call, Gracie. Personally, I *hate* Christmas. And I'd prefer to be sitting under a palm tree right now, but hey, here I am. So let's get on with it."

"My name's not Gracie."

"Whatever." He looked around. "Where's your tree? You're supposed to have a stupid Christmas tree."

"I haven't had time to buy a tree. There's this guy I'm trying to find. Sandy Claws. He's wanted for burglary, and now he's failed to appear for his court appearance, so he's in violation of his bond agreement."

"Hah! Good one. That's a prizewinning excuse for not having a Christmas tree. Let me see if I've got the details right. You're a bounty hunter?"

"Yes."

"You don't look like a bounty hunter."

"What's a bounty hunter supposed to look like?"

"Dressed in black, six-shooter strapped to your leg, a cheroot clenched between your teeth."

I did another eye roll.

"And you're after Santa Claus because he skipped."

"Not Santa Claus," I said. "Sandy Claws. *S-a-n-d-y C-l-a-w-s.*"

"Sandy Claws. Cripes, how would you like to have *that* name? What'd he steal, kitty litter?"

This was coming from a guy named for a train engine. "First, I have a legitimate job. I work for Vincent Plum Bail Bonds as a bond enforcement agent. Second, Claws isn't such a weird name. It was probably Klaus and got screwed up at Ellis Island. It happened a lot. Third, I don't know why I'm explaining this to you. Probably I had a stroke and fell down and hit my head and I'm actually in ICU right now, hallucinating all this."

"You see, this is typical of the problem. Nobody believes in the mystical anymore. Nobody believes in miracles. As it happens, I'm a little supernatural. Why can't you just accept that and go with it? I bet you don't believe in Santa Claus either. Maybe Sandy Claws didn't have his name changed from Klaus. Maybe he had his name changed from Santa Claus. Maybe the old guy got tired of the toys-for-kids routine and just wanted to go hide out somewhere."

"So you think Santa Claus might be living in Trenton under an assumed name?"

Diesel shrugged. "It's possible. Santa's a pretty shifty guy. He has a dark side, you know."

"I didn't know that."

"Not many people know that. So if you could catch this Claws guy, you'd get a Christmas tree?"

"Probably not. I haven't got money for a tree. And I haven't got any ornaments."

"Oh man, I'm stuck with a whiner. No time, no money, no ornaments. Yada, yada, yada."

"Hey, it's my life and I don't have to have a Christmas tree if I don't want one."

Actually, I really did want a Christmas tree.

I wanted a big fat tree with bright colored lights and an angel on top. I wanted a wreath on my front door. I wanted red candlesticks on my dining room table. I wanted my closet filled with beautifully wrapped presents for my family. I wanted Christmas music playing on my stereo. And I wanted a fruitcake in my refrigerator. It was what every red-blooded Plum was supposed to have at Christmas, right?

I wanted to wake up in the morning and feel happy and filled with good cheer and peace on earth and good will toward men. And I wanted to have a partridge in my pear tree.

Well, guess what? I didn't have *any* of those things. No tree? no wreath, no candlesticks, no presents, no freaking fruitcake, and no god-damn partridge.

Every year I chased after the perfect Christmas and every year Christmas barely happened. My Christmases were always a mess of badly wrapped last-minute presents, a chunk of fruitcake sent home in a doggy bag from my parents' house, and for the last couple years I haven't had a tree. I just couldn't seem to *get to* Christmas.

"What do you mean, you don't want a Christmas tree?" Diesel said. "Everyone wants a Christmas tree. If you had a Christmas tree,

Santa would bring you stuff . . . like hair curlers and slut shoes."

A sigh escaped. "I appreciate your insight into Christmas, but you're going to have to leave now. I have things to do. I have to work on the Claws case and then later I promised my mother I'd be over to bake Christmas cookies."

"Not a good plan. Baking cookies doesn't do a lot for me. I have a better plan. How about we find Claws and then we shop for a tree? And on the way home from the tree shopping we can see if the Titans are playing tonight. Maybe we can catch a hockey game."

"How do you know about the Titans?"

"I know everything."

I did yet another eye roll and brushed past him. I was doing so many eye rolls, they were giving me a headache.

"Okay, so I've been to Trenton before," he said. "You've got to stop doing those eye rolls. You're going to shake something loose in there."

I'd planned to take a shower, but there was no way I was getting into the shower with a strange man sitting in my living room. "I'm changing my clothes, and then I'm going to work. You aren't going to pop into my bedroom, are you?"

"Do you want me to?"

"No!"

"Your loss." He returned to the couch and television. "Let me know if you change your mind."

An hour later we were in my Honda CRV. Me and Supernatural Man. I hadn't invited him to ride along with me. He'd simply unlocked the door and gotten into the car.

"Admit it, you're getting to like me, right?" he asked.

"Wrong, I *don't* like you. But, for some unfathomable reason, I'm not totally freaked out."

"It's because I'm charming."

"You are *not* charming. You're a jerk."

He flashed another one of the killer smiles at me. "Yeah, but I'm a *charming* jerk."

I was driving and Diesel was riding shotgun, flipping through my folder on Claws. "So what do we do here, go to his house and drag him out?"

"He's living with his sister, Elaine Gluck. I stopped by their house yesterday, and his sister said he'd disappeared. I think she knows where he is so I'm going back today to put some pressure on her."

"Seventy-six years old, and this guy broke into Kreider's Hardware at two in the morning and stole fifteen hundred dollars' worth of power tools and a gallon of Morning Glory yellow paint," Diesel read. "Got caught on a security camera. What an idiot. Everybody knows you've got to wear a ski mask when you pull a job like that. Doesn't he watch television? Doesn't he go to the movies?" Diesel pulled out a file photo. "Hold the phone. Is this the guy?"

"Yes."

Diesel's face brightened and the smile returned. "And you stopped by his house yesterday?"

"Yes."

"Are you any good at what you do? Are you good at tracking down people?"

"No. But I'm lucky."

"Even better," he said.

"You look like you've had a revelation."

"Big time. The pieces are beginning to fit together."

"And?"

"Sorry," he said. "It was one of those personal revelations."

SANDY CLAWS AND his sister, Elaine Gluck, lived in North Trenton in a neighborhood of small houses, big televisions, and American-made cars. Holiday spirit ran high in Sandy's neighborhood. Porches were trimmed in colored lights. Electric candles glowed in windows. Postage-stamp front yards were crammed with reindeer, Frosties, and Santas. Sandy Claws' house was the best, or the worst, depending on your point of view. The house was blanketed in red, green, yellow, and blue Christmas lights, interspersed with waterfalls of tiny white twinkle lights. A lighted sign on the roof blinked the message PEACE ON EARTH. A large plastic Santa and his sleigh were stuffed into the minuscule front yard. And three plastic, five-foot-tall Dickens-era carolers huddled together on the front porch.

"Now this is spirit," Diesel said. "Nice touch with the blinking lights on the roof."

"At the risk of being cynical, probably he stole the lights."

"Not my problem," Diesel said, opening the car door.

"Hold it. Close the door," I said. "*You* stay *here* while I talk to Elaine."

"And miss out on all the fun? No way." He angled out of the CRV, and he stood, hands in pockets, on the sidewalk, waiting for me.

"Okay. Fine. Just don't say anything. Just stand behind me and try to look respectable."

"You think I don't look respectable?"

"You have gravy stains on your shirt."

He looked down at himself. "This is my favorite shirt. It's real comfy. And they're not gravy stains. They're grease stains. I used to work on my bike in this shirt."

"What kind of bike?"

"Customized Harley. I had a big old cruiser with Python pipes." He smiled, remembering. "It was sweet."

"What happened to it?"

"Crashed it."

"Is that how you got the way you are now? Dead, or something?"

"No. The only thing that died was the bike."

It was midmorning and the sun was lost behind cloud cover that was the color and texture of bean curd. I was wearing wool socks, thick-soled CAT boots, black jeans, a red plaid flannel shirt over a T-shirt, and a black leather biker jacket. I looked pretty damn tough, in a very cool way . . . and I was freezing my ass off. Diesel was wearing his jacket unzipped and didn't look the least bit cold.

I crossed the street and rang the doorbell.

Elaine opened the door wide and smiled out at me. She was a couple inches shorter than me and almost as wide as she was tall. She was maybe seventy years old. Her hair was snow white, cut short and curled. She had apple cheeks and bright blue eyes. And she smelled like gingerbread cookies. "Hello, dear," she said, "how nice to see you again." She looked to the side where Diesel was lurking and gasped. "Oh my," she said, red scald rising from her neck to her cheek. "You startled me. I didn't see you standing there at first."

"I'm with Ms. Plum," Diesel said. "I'm her . . . assistant."

"Goodness."

"Is Sandy at home?" I asked.

"I'm afraid not," she said. "He's very busy at this time of year. Sometimes I don't see him for days on end. He owns a toy store, you know. And toy stores are very busy at Christmas."

I knew the toy store. It was a shabby little store in a strip mall in Hamilton Township. "I stopped by the store yesterday," I said. "It was closed."

"Sandy must have been busy running errands. Sometimes he closes down to run errands."

"Elaine, you used this house as collateral to bond out your brother. If Sandy doesn't appear in court, my employer will seize this house."

Elaine continued to smile. "I'm sure your employer wouldn't do a mean thing like that. Sandy and I just moved here, but already we love this house. We wallpapered the bathroom last week. It looks lovely."

Oh boy. This was going to be a disaster. If I don't bring Claws in, I don't get paid and I look like a big failure. If I threaten and intimidate Elaine into ratting on her brother, I feel like a jerk. Better to be after a crazed killer who's hated by everyone, including his mother. Of course, crazed killers tend to shoot at bounty hunters, and getting shot at isn't high on my list of favorite activities.

"I smell gingerbread," Diesel said to Elaine. "I bet you're baking cookies."

"I bake cookies every day," she told him. "Yesterday I made sugar cookies with colored sprinkles and today I'm making gingerbread."

"I love gingerbread," Diesel said. He slid past Elaine and found his way to her kitchen. He selected a cookie from a plate heaped with cookies, took a bite, and smiled. "I bet you add vinegar to your cookie dough."

"It's my secret ingredient," Elaine said.

"So where is the old guy?" Diesel asked. "Where's Sandy?"

"He's probably at his workshop. He makes a lot of his own toys, you know."

Diesel wandered to the back door and looked out. "And where's the workshop?"

"There's a small workshop behind the store.

And then there's the main workshop. I don't know exactly where the main workshop is. I've never been there. I'm always too busy with the cookies."

"Is it in Trenton?" Diesel asked.

Elaine looked thoughtful. "Isn't that something?" she said. "I don't know. Sandy talks about the toys and about the labor problem, but I can't remember him ever talking about the workshop."

Diesel took a cookie for the road, thanked Elaine, and we left.

"Want some of my cookie?" Diesel asked, the cookie held between perfect white teeth while he clicked the seat belt into place.

"I do not."

He had a nice voice. Slightly husky and hinting of a smile. His eyes fit the voice. I really hated that I liked the voice and the eyes. My life is already complicated by two men. One is my mentor and tormentor, a Cuban-American bounty hunter/businessman named Ranger. He was currently out of town. No one knew where he was or when he'd return. This was normal. The other man in my life is a Trenton cop named Joe Morelli. When I was a kid, Morelli lured me into his father's garage and taught me how to play choo-choo. I was the tunnel and Morelli was the train, if you get the picture. When I was a teen working at Tasty Pastry Bakery, Morelli sweet-talked me onto the floor after hours and performed a more adult version of choo-choo behind the éclair case. We've both grown up some since then. The attraction is still there. It's been enhanced by genuine affection . . . maybe even love. We haven't totally mastered trust and the ability to commit. I really didn't need a third *potentially nonhuman* guy in my life.

"I bet you're worried about the way those jeans are fitting, right?" Diesel asked. "Afraid to add cookie calories?"

"Wrong! My jeans fit just fine." I didn't want a cookie with Diesel spit on it. I mean, what do I know about him? And okay, so my jeans actually were a little tight. Yeesh.

He bit off the gingerbread man's head. "What's next? Does Claws have kids we can interrogate? I think I'm getting the hang of this."

"No kids. I ran a check on him, and he has no relatives in the area. Same with Elaine. She's widowed with no children."

"That must be hard on Elaine. A woman gets those urges, you know."

I narrowed my eyes. "Urges?"

"Kids. Procreation. Maternal urges."

"Who *are* you?"

"That's a good question," Diesel said. "I'm not sure I fully know the answer to that. Do any of us truly know who we are?"

Great. Now he's a philosopher.

"Don't you have maternal urges?" he asked. "Don't you hear that biological clock ticking? Tick, tick, tick," he said, smiling again, having some fun with it.

"I have a hamster."

"Hey, you couldn't ask for more than that. Hamsters are cool. Personally, I think kids are overrated."

I was getting an eye twitch. I put my finger to my eye to stop the fluttering. "I'd rather not get into this right now."

Diesel held his hands up. "No problemo. Don't want to make you uncomfortable."

Yeah, right.

"Back to the big manhunt. Have you got a plan here?" he asked.

"I'm going back to the store. I didn't realize there was a workshop attached."

Twenty minutes later we stood at the front door to the store, staring at the small, hand-written cardboard sign in the window. CLOSED. Diesel put his hand to the doorknob and the locks tumbled open.

"Pretty impressive, hunh?" he said.

"Pretty illegal."

He pushed the door open. "You're a real spoilsport, you know that?"

We both squinted into the dark. The only windows were the small panes of glass in the door. The shop was about the size of a two-car garage. Diesel closed the door behind us and flipped a light switch. Two overhead fluorescent fixtures buzzed on and threw a dim, flickering light across the interior.

"Boy, this is cheery," Diesel said. "This would make me want to buy toys. Right after I poked my eye out and slit my throat."

The walls were lined with shelves, but the shelves were empty, and train sets, board games, dolls, action figures, and stuffed animals were all jumbled together on the floor.

"This is strange," I said. "Why are the toys on the floor?"

Diesel looked around the room. "Maybe someone had a temper tantrum." An ancient cash register sat on a small counter. Diesel punched a key and the register opened. "Seven dollars and fifty cents," he said. "Don't think Sandy does much business." He walked the length of the store and tested the back door. The door was unlocked. He opened the door and we both peeked into the back room. "Not much to see here, either," Diesel said.

There were a couple of long, metal folding

tables and several metal folding chairs. Crude wood toys in various stages of completion cluttered the tables. Most were clunky carved animals and even clunkier carved trains. The train cars were connected by large hooks and eyes.

"Look around for something that might have the address of the other workshop," I said. "It might be printed on a shipping label or box. Or maybe there's a scrap of paper with a phone number."

We worked both rooms, but we didn't find an address or phone number. The only item in the trash was a crumpled bakery bag from Baldanno's. Sandy Claws had a sweet tooth. The store didn't have a phone. None had been listed on the bond agreement and we didn't see any on site. The bond agreement also didn't list a cell phone. That didn't guarantee that one didn't exist.

We left the store, locking the front door behind us. We stood beside my CRV in the parking lot and looked back. "Do you notice anything odd about this store?" I asked Diesel.

"No name," Diesel said. "There's just a door with a small cutout of a wooden soldier on it."

"What kind of a toy store doesn't have a name?"

"If you look closely you can see where the

sign was torn off," Diesel said. "It used to hang above the door."

"Probably this is a front for a numbers operation."

Diesel shook his head. "It would have phones. It would probably have a computer. There'd be ashtrays and cigarette butts."

I raised my eyebrows at him.

"I watch television," he said.

Okay. Whatever. "I'm going to my parents' now," I told him. "Maybe you want me to drop you someplace. Shopping center, pool hall, loony bin . . ."

"Boy, that really hurts. You don't want me to meet your parents."

"It's not like we're going steady."

"My assignment is to bring you some Christmas cheer, and I take my job *very* seriously."

I gave him disgusted. "You do *not* take your job seriously. You told me you don't even like Christmas."

"I was caught by surprise. It's not usually my gig. But I'm starting to get into it. Can't you tell? Don't I look more cheery?"

"I'm not going to get rid of you, am I?"

He rocked back on his heels, hands in jacket pockets, a large grin firmly in place. "No."

I blew out a sigh, put the car into gear, and pulled out of the lot. It wasn't a far ride to my parents' house in the Burg. The Burg is short for Chambersburg, a small residential community that sits on the edge of Trenton proper. I was born and raised in the Burg and I'll be a Burger for life. I've tried moving away, but I can't seem to get far enough.

Like most houses in the Burg, my parents' house is a small two-story clapboard built on a small, narrow lot. And like many houses in the Burg, the house shares a common wall with an identical house. Mabel Markowitz owns the house that adjoins my parents' house. She lives there alone, now that her husband has passed on. She keeps her windows clean, she plays bingo twice a week at the senior center, and she squeezes thirteen cents out of every dime.

I parked at the curb and Diesel looked at the two houses. Mrs. Markowitz's house was painted a bilious green. She had a plaster statue of the Virgin Mary in her tiny front yard and she'd put a pot of plastic red poinsettias next to the Virgin. A lone candle had been placed in her front window. My parents' house was painted yellow and brown and was decorated with a string of colored lights across the front of the house. A big old plastic Santa, his red suit sun-bleached to pale pink, had been set up in my parents' front yard, in direct competition with Mrs. Markowitz's Virgin. My mother had electric candles in all the windows and a wreath on the front door.

"Holy crap," Diesel said. "This is a car crash."

I had to agree with him. The houses were fascinating in their awfulness. Even worse, they were a comfort. They'd looked exactly like this for as long as I could remember. I couldn't imagine them looking any other way. When I was fourteen Mrs. Markowitz's Virgin had gotten beaned with a baseball and some of her head had chipped away, but that didn't stop the Virgin from blessing the house. She stood stalwart through wind and rain and sleet and storm with a chipped head. Just as Santa faded and dented but returned each year.

Grandma Mazur was behind my parents' glass storm door, looking out at us. Grandma Mazur lives with my parents now that Grampa Mazur's eating pork rinds and deep-fried peanut butter sandwiches with Elvis. Grandma Mazur's mostly spindle bone and slack skin. She keeps her gray hair curled tight to her head and carries a .45 long barrel in her purse. The concept of growing old gracefully has never taken hold with Grandma.

Grandma opened the door when I approached with Diesel. "Who's this?" she asked, eyeballing Diesel. "I didn't know you were bringing a new man over. Look at me. I'm not even dressed up. And what about Joseph? What happened to him?"

"Who's Joseph?" Diesel wanted to know.

"He's her boyfriend," Grandma Mazur said. "Joseph Morelli. He's a Trenton cop. He's supposed to be coming over later for dinner on account of it's Sunday."

Diesel grinned down at me. "You didn't tell me you had a boyfriend."

I introduced Diesel to my mom, Grandma Mazur, and my dad.

"What's with men and ponytails?" my father said. "Girls are supposed to have long hair. Men are supposed to have short hair."

"What about Jesus?" Grandma asked. "He had long hair."

"This guy isn't Jesus," my father said. He stuck his hand out to Diesel. "Nice to meet you. What are you, one of them wrestlers or something?"

"No sir, I'm not a wrestler," Diesel said, smiling.

"They're sports entertainers," Grandma said. "Only some of them are real good at wrestling, like Kurt Angle and Lance Storm."

"Lance Storm?" my father said. "What kind of a name is that?"

"It's one of those Canadian names," Grandma said. "He's a cutie, too."

Diesel looked at me and the smile widened. "I love your family."

TWO

MY SISTER VALERIE came in from the kitchen. Valerie is recently divorced and penniless and has moved herself and her two kids into my old bedroom. Before the divorce and the move back to Jersey, Valerie was living in southern California where she had limited success at cloning herself into Meg Ryan. Valerie's still got the blond shag. The resilient perkiness dropped out of her somewhere over Kansas on the flight home.

"Dang," Valerie said, taking Diesel in.

Grandma agreed. "He's a pip, isn't he?" she said. "He's a real looker."

Diesel elbowed me in the side. "You see? They like me."

I dragged Diesel into the living room. "They think you've got a nice ass. That's different from liking you. Sit in front of the television.

Watch cartoons. Try to find a ball game. Don't talk to anybody."

My mother and grandmother and sister were waiting for me in the kitchen.

"Who is he?" Valerie wanted to know. "He's gorgeous."

"Yeah, and I can tell he's a hottie," Grandma said. "He's got that look in his eye. And I bet he's got a good package."

"He's nobody," I said, trying to push aside thoughts of Diesel's package. "He moved into the building, and he doesn't know anybody, so I've sort of adopted him. He's kind of a charity case."

Valerie got serious. "Is he married?"

"I don't think so, but you don't want him. He's not normal."

"He looks normal."

"Trust me. *He's not your normal guy.*"

"He's gay, right?"

"Yep. That's it. I think he's gay." Better than telling Valerie that Diesel was a supernatural pain in the behind.

"The gorgeous ones are always gay," Valerie said with a sigh. "It's a rule."

Grandma had a big wad of cookie dough on the table. She rolled it out and then she gave me a star-shaped cookie cutter. "You do the sugar cookies," Grandma said. "I'm going to get Valerie working on the drop cookies."

If I take anything with me when I die it'll be the way my mother's kitchen smells. Coffee brewing in the morning, red cabbage and pot roast steaming the kitchen windows on a cold day in February, a hot apple pie on the counter in September. Sounds corny when I think about it, but the smells are real and as much a part of me as my thumb and my heart. I swear I first smelled pineapple upside-down cake when I was in the womb.

Today the air in my mother's kitchen was heavy with butter cookies baking in the oven. My mom used real butter and real vanilla, and the vanilla scent clung to my skin and hung in my hair. The kitchen was warm and cluttered with women, and I was drunk on butter cookies. It would be a perfect moment, if only there wasn't a space alien sitting in the living room, watching television with my dad.

I stuck my head out the kitchen door and looked through the dining room to Diesel and my dad in the living room. Diesel was standing in front of the Christmas tree—a scrawny, five-foot-tall spruce set into a rickety stand. Four days to Christmas and already the tree was dropping needles. My father had placed a green and silver foil star at the balding top of the tree. The rest of the tree was ringed with colored twinkle lights and decorated with an assortment of ornaments collected over the lifetime of my parents' marriage. The rickety stand was wrapped in white cotton batting that was supposed to resemble snow. A village of aging cardboard houses had been assembled on the cotton batting.

Valerie's kids, nine-year-old Angie and seven-year-old Mary Alice, had finished the tree off with gobs of tinsel. Angie is the perfect child and is often mistaken for a very short forty-year-old woman. Mary Alice has had a longstanding identity problem and is usually convinced she's a horse.

"Nice tree," Diesel said.

My father concentrated on the television screen. My father knew a loser tree when he saw one and this was no prizewinner. He'd cheaped out, as usual, and he'd gotten the tree from Andy at the Mobil station. Andy's trees always looked like they were grown next to a nuclear power plant.

Mary Alice and Angie had been watching television with my father. Mary Alice tore her attention away from the screen and looked up at Diesel. "Who are you?" she asked.

"My name's Diesel," he said. "Who are you?"

"I'm Mary Alice, and I'm a beautiful palomino. And that's my sister Angie. She's just a girl."

"You aren't a palomino," Angie said. "Palominos have golden hair, and you have brown hair."

"I can be a palomino if I want to," Mary Alice said.

"Can not."

"Can too."

"Can not."

I closed the kitchen door and returned to the cookie cutting. "There's a toy store in the Price Cutter strip mall in Hamilton Township," I said to my mother and grandmother. "Do either of you know anything about it?"

"I never saw a toy store there," Grandma said, "but I was shopping with Tootie Frick last week, and we saw a store with a toy soldier on the door. I tried the door, but it was locked, and there weren't any lights on inside. I asked someone about it and he said the store was haunted. He said last week there was an electrical storm *inside* the store, with thunder and everything."

I transferred a raw cookie-dough star from the table to the cookie sheet. "I don't know about the haunted part, but the place is supposed to be a toy store. The guy who owns it has failed to appear for a court date, and I haven't been able to find him. Supposedly he makes some of his own toys, and he has a workshop somewhere, but I haven't been able to get an address for the workshop."

When the bail bonds office opened tomorrow morning I'd have Connie, the office manager, run a cyber search on Claws. I could also check to see if Claws was on the books for electric and water at a location other than his house and his store.

"You're gonna have to pick the pace up here," Grandma said. "We still got to put the frosting on these cookies. And we got the filled cookies to make yet. And the cream cheese snowballs. I can't be doing this all day because I gotta go to a viewing tonight. Lenny Jelinek is laid out. He was a member of the Moose lodge, and you know what that means."

My mother and I looked at Grandma. We were clueless.

"I give up," my mother said. "What does that mean?"

"There's always a crowd when there's a Moose laid out. Lots of men. Easy pickins, if you're in the market for a studmuffin."

My mother was mixing cookie dough in a big bowl. She looked up, spoon in hand, and a glob of dough slid off the spoon and plopped onto the floor. "Studmuffin?"

"Of course, I've already got my studmuffin all picked out," Grandma said. "I met him at Harry Farfel's viewing, week before last. It was a real romantic meeting. My studmuffin just moved into the area. He was driving around, trying to find a business associate, and he got lost. So he went into Stiva's Funeral Parlor to ask for directions, and he bumped right into me. He said he bumped into me on account of he has vision problems, but I knew it was fate. All the little hairs on my arm stood up the second he knocked me down. Can you imagine? And now we're practically going steady. He's a real honey. He's a good kisser, too. Makes my lips tingle!"

"You never said anything," my mother said.

"I didn't want to make a fuss, what with Christmas on top of us."

I thought it was sort of cool that Grandma had a studmuffin, but I didn't really want a mental image of Grandma and the good kisser. Last time Grandma brought a man home to dinner he took his glass eye out at the table and set it alongside his spoon while he ate.

I had some success at eliminating senior studmuffin thoughts. I was having less success at eliminating thoughts of Diesel. I was worried he was in the living room deciding who in my family should be beamed up to the mothership. Or maybe he wasn't an alien. What then? Maybe he was Satan. Except, he didn't smell like fire and brimstone. His scent was more *yum*. Okay, probably he wasn't Satan. I went to the kitchen door and did another look out.

The kids were on the floor, transfixed by the television. My father was in his chair, sleeping. No Diesel. "Hey," I shouted to Angie. "Where's Diesel?"

Angie shrugged. Mary Alice looked around at me and also shrugged.

"Dad," I shouted. "Where'd Diesel go?"

My dad opened one eye. "Out. He said he'd be back by dinnertime."

Out? As in *out for a walk*? Or out as in *out of body*? I looked up to the ceiling, hoping Diesel wasn't hovering above us like the Ghost of Christmas Past. "Did he say where he was going?"

"Nope. Just said he'd be back." My father's eyes closed. End of conversation.

I suddenly had a scary thought. I ran to the front foyer with the spatula still in my hand. I looked out the front door and my heart momentarily stopped. The CRV was gone. He took my car. "Damn, damn, damn!" I went outside to the sidewalk and looked up and down the street. "Diesel!" I yelled. *"Deeezel!"*

No response. Big deal Man of Mysterious Talents can open doors but can't hear me calling him.

"I just got to thinking about today's paper," Grandma said when I returned to the kitchen. "I was looking at the want ads this morning, thinking I could use a job if the right thing turned up . . . like being a bar singer. Anyway, I didn't see any ads for bar singers, but there was an ad in there for toy makers. It was worded real cute, too. It said they were looking for elves."

The paper was on the floor beside my father's chair. I found the paper and read through the want ads. Sure enough, there was an ad for toy makers. Elves preferred. A phone number was given. Applicants were told to ask for Lester.

I dialed the number and got Lester on the second ring.

"Here's the thing, Lester," I said. "I got this phone number out of the paper. Are you really hiring toy makers?"

"Yes, but we're only taking toy makers of the very highest caliber."

"Elves?"

"Everyone knows, they're the top of the line toy makers."

"Are you taking on anyone other than elves?"

"Are you a non-elf, looking for a job?"

"I'm looking for a toy maker. Sandy Claws."

Click. Disconnect. I redialed and someone other than Lester answered. I asked for Lester and was told Lester wasn't available. I asked for the job seeker interview location and this resulted in another disconnect.

"I didn't know we had elves in Trenton," Grandma said. "Isn't that something? Elves right under our nose."

"I think he was kidding about the elves," I said.

"Too bad," Grandma said. "Elves would be fun."

"You're always working," my mother said to me. "You can't even bake Christmas cookies without making phone calls about criminals. Loretta Krakowski's daughter doesn't do that. Loretta's daughter comes home from the button factory and never thinks about her job. Loretta's daughter handmade all her own Christmas cards." My mother stopped mixing dough and looked at me, wide-eyed and fear-filled. "Did you send out your Christmas cards?"

Omigod, Christmas cards. I forgot all about Christmas cards. "Sure," I said. "I sent them out last week." I hoped God and Santa Claus weren't listening to me fib.

My mother blew out a whoosh of air and made the sign of the cross. "Thank goodness. I was afraid you forgot, again."

Mental note. Buy some Christmas cards.

By five o'clock we were done with the cookies and my mother had a tray of lasagna in the oven. The cookies were in cookie jars and cookie tins and some were stacked high on plates for instant eating. I was at the sink, washing the last of the baking sheets, and I felt the skin prickle at the back of my neck. I turned and bumped into Diesel.

"You took my car," I said, jumping back. "You just drove off with it. You *stole* it!"

"Chill. I *borrowed* it. I didn't want to disturb you. You were busy with the cookie making."

"If you had to go somewhere why didn't you just pop yourself there . . . like you popped into my apartment?"

"I'm keeping a low profile. I save the popping for special occasions."

"You're not really the Spirit of Christmas, are you?"

"I could be if I wanted. I hear the job's up for grabs."

He was wearing the same boots and jeans and jacket, but he'd substituted a brown sweater for the stained thermal.

"Did you go home to change?"

"Home is far away." He playfully twirled a lock of my hair around his finger. "You ask a lot of questions."

"Yeah, but I'm not getting any answers."

"There's a chubby little guy in the living room with your dad. Is that your boyfriend?"

"That's Albert Kloughn. He's Valerie's boyfriend."

I heard the front door open, and seconds later, Morelli sauntered into the kitchen. He looked first to me and then to Diesel. He extended his hand to Diesel. "Joe Morelli," he said.

"Diesel."

They spent a moment measuring. Diesel was an inch taller and had more bulk. Morelli wasn't someone you'd want to meet in a dark alley. Morelli was all lean hard muscle and dark assessing eyes. The moment passed, Morelli smiled at me and dropped a feather-light kiss on the top of my head.

"Diesel is an alien or something," I said to Morelli. "He appeared in my kitchen this morning."

"As long as he didn't spend the night," Morelli said. He reached around me to a cookie tin, removed the lid, and selected a cookie.

I cut my eyes to Diesel and caught him smiling.

Morelli's pager buzzed. He checked the readout and swore to himself. He used the kitchen phone, staring at his shoes while he was talking. Never a good sign. The conversation was short.

"I have to go," Morelli said. "Work."

"Will I see you later?"

Morelli pulled me out to the back stoop and shut the kitchen door behind us. "Stanley Komenski was just found stuffed into an industrial waste barrel. It was sitting in the alley behind that new Thai restaurant on Sumner Street. Apparently it had been sitting there for days and was attracting flies, not to mention some local dogs and a pack of crows. He was muscle for Lou Two Toes so this is going to get ugly. And if that isn't bad enough, there's something screwy going on with the electric grid. There have been power outages in pockets all over Trenton and they all of a sudden correct themselves. Not a big deal, but it's making a mess out of traffic." Morelli turned his head to look through the glass pane, into the kitchen. "Who's the big guy?"

"I told you. He popped into my kitchen this morning. I think he's an alien. Or maybe he's some kind of a ghost."

Morelli felt my forehead. "Are you running a fever? Have you fallen down again?"

"I'm fine. Pay attention. The guy popped into my kitchen."

"Yeah, but *everyone* pops into your kitchen."

"Not like this. He really popped in. Like he was beamed down, or something."

"Okay," Morelli said, "I believe you. He's an alien." Morelli dragged me tight against him, and he kissed me. And he left.

"So," Diesel said, when I returned to the kitchen. "How'd that go?"

"I don't think he believed me."

"No kidding. You go around telling people I'm an alien and they're eventually going to lock you up in the booby hatch. And just for the record, I'm not an alien. And I'm not a ghost."

"Vampire?"

"A vampire can't enter a home without an invitation."

"This is too weird."

"It's not that weird," Diesel said. "I can do some things most people can't do. Don't make more of it than it is."

"*I don't know what it is!*"

Diesel's smile returned.

AT PRECISELY SIX o'clock we sat down to the table.

"Isn't this nice," Grandma said. "It feels like a party."

"I'm squished," Mary Alice said. "Horses don't like when they're squished. There's too many people at this table."

"I've got room," Albert Kloughn said. "I can pick my fork up and everything."

My father already had lasagna on his plate. My father always got served first with the hope that he'd be busy eating and wouldn't jump up and strangle Grandma Mazur. "Where's the gravy?" he asked. "Where's the extra sauce?"

Angie carefully passed the bowl with the extra marinara sauce to Mary Alice. Mary Alice had a hard time getting her hooves around the bowl, the bowl wobbled in midair and then crashed onto the table, setting loose a tidal wave of tomato sauce. Grandma reached across the table to grab the bowl, knocked over a candlestick and the tablecloth went up in flames. This wasn't the first time this had happened.

"*Yow!* Fire," Kloughn yelled. "Fire. *Fire!* We're all gonna die!"

My father looked up briefly, shook his head like he couldn't believe this was actually his life, and returned to shoveling in his lasagna. My mother made the sign of the cross. And I dumped a pitcher of ice water into the middle of the table, putting an end to the fire.

Diesel grinned. "I love this family. I just *love* this family."

"I didn't really think we were going to die," Kloughn said.

"Have another slice of lasagna," my mother said to Valerie. "Look at you, you're all skin and bones."

"That's because she throws up when she eats," Grandma said.

"I have a virus," Valerie said. "I get nervous."

"Maybe you're pregnant," Grandma said. "Maybe you got the morning sickness all day long."

Kloughn went white and fell off his chair. *Crash*, onto the floor.

Grandma looked down at him. "They don't make men like they used to."

Valerie clapped her hand to her mouth and ran out of the room, up the stairs to the bathroom.

"Holy Mary Mother of God," my mother said.

Kloughn opened his eyes. "What happened?"

"You fainted," Grandma said. "You went down like a sack of sand."

Diesel got out of his chair and helped

Kloughn to his feet. "Way to go, stud," Diesel said.

"Thank you," Kloughn said. "I'm very virile. It runs in the family."

"I'm tired of sitting here," Mary Alice said. "I need to gallop."

"You will not gallop," my mother yelled at Mary Alice. "You're not a horse. You're a little girl, and you'll act like one or you'll go to your room."

We all sat stunned because my mother never yelled. And even more shocking, my mother (having put her time in with me, the original space cadet) never made an issue of the horse thing.

There was a moment of silence and then Mary Alice started bawling. She had her eyes scrunched tight and her mouth wide open. Her face was red and blotchy and tears dripped off her cheeks onto her shirt.

"Christ," my father said. "Somebody do something."

"Hey, kid," Diesel said to Mary Alice, "what do you want for Christmas this year?"

Mary Alice tried to stop crying but her breath was coming in gulps and hiccups. She scrubbed tears off her face and wiped her nose with the back of her hand. "I don't want anything for Christmas. I *hate* Christmas. Christmas is poopy."

"There must be something you want," Grandma said.

Mary Alice pushed her food around on her plate with her fork. "There's nothing. And I know there's no Santa Claus, too. He's just a big fat fake."

No one had an immediate response. She'd caught us by surprise. *There was no Santa Claus.* How crappy is that?

Diesel finally leaned forward on his elbows and looked across the table at Mary Alice. "This is the way I see it, Mary Alice. I can't say for sure if there's really a Santa Claus, but I think it's fun to pretend. The truth is, we all have a choice to make, and we can believe in whatever we want."

"I think you're poopy, too," Mary Alice said to Diesel.

Diesel slid his arm across my shoulders and leaned close, his breath warm against my ear. "You were smart to choose a hamster," he said.

Valerie returned to the dining room in time for dessert. "It's an allergy," she said. "I think I'm lactose-intolerant."

"Boy, that's a shame," Grandma said. "We got pineapple upside-down cake for tonight, and it's got lots of whipped cream on it."

Beads of sweat appeared on Valerie's upper lip and forehead, and Valerie ran back upstairs.

"Funny how these things come on," Grandma said. "She was never lactose-intolerant before. She must have caught it in California."

"I'm going to get some cookies from the kitchen," my mother said.

I followed after her and found her belting back a tumbler of Four Roses.

She jumped when she saw me. "You startled me," she said.

"I came to help with the cookies."

"I was just taking a nip." A shudder raced through my mother. "It's Christmas, you know."

This was a nip the size of a Big Gulp. "Probably Valerie isn't pregnant," I said.

My mother drained the Big Gulp, crossed herself, and went back into the dining room with the cookies.

"So," Grandma said to Kloughn, "do you make Christmas cookies at your house? Is your tree up yet?"

"We don't actually have a tree," Kloughn said. "We're Jewish."

Everyone stopped eating, even my father.

"You don't look Jewish," Grandma said. "You don't wear one of them beanies."

Kloughn rolled his eyes up as if looking for his missing beanie, clearly at a loss for words, probably still not getting total oxygen to his brain after fainting.

"How great is this?" Grandma said. "If you marry Valerie we can celebrate some of those Jewish holidays. And we can get a set of the candlesticks. I always wanted one of those Jewish candlestick things. Isn't this something," Grandma said. "Wait until I tell the girls at the beauty parlor that we might get a Jew in our family. Everyone's going to be jealous."

My father was still sitting lost in thought. His daughter might marry a Jewish guy. This wasn't a great thing to happen, in my father's view. Not that he had anything against Jewish guys. It was that chances were slim to nonexistent that Kloughn was Italian. In my father's scheme of things, there were Italians and then there was the rest of the world. "You wouldn't be of Italian descent, would you?" my father asked Kloughn.

"My grandparents were German," Kloughn said.

My father sighed and went back to concentrating on his lasagna. Yet another fuckup in the family.

My mother was white-faced. Bad enough her daughters didn't attend church. The possibility of non-Catholic grandchildren was a disaster right up there with nuclear annihilation. "Maybe I need to put a couple more cookies on the plate," my mother said, pushing back from the table.

One more cookie run and my mother was going to be passed out on the kitchen floor.

At nine o'clock Angie and Mary Alice were tucked into bed. My grandmother was somewhere with her studmuffin, and my mother and father were in front of the television. Valerie and Albert Kloughn were *discussing* things in the kitchen. And Diesel and I were standing outside on the sidewalk in front of the CRV. It was cold and our breath made frost clouds.

"So what happens now?" I asked. "Do you get beamed back up?"

"Not tonight. Couldn't get a flight."

My eyebrows raised a quarter of an inch.

"I'm kidding," he said. "Boy, you'll believe anything."

Apparently. "Well, it's been a real treat," I said, "but I've got to go now."

"Sure. See you around."

I got into the CRV, cranked the engine over, and took off. When I got to the corner I swiveled in my seat and looked back. Diesel was still standing exactly where I'd left him. I drove around the block, and when I returned to my parents' house the sidewalk was empty. Diesel had vanished without a trace.

He didn't pop into my car when I was half-way home. He didn't appear in my apartment building hallway. He wasn't in my kitchen, bedroom, or bathroom.

I dropped a piece of butter cookie into the hamster cage on my kitchen counter and watched Rex jump off his wheel and rush at the cookie. "We got rid of the alien," I said to Rex. "Good deal, hunh?"

Rex looked like he was thinking, *alien schmalien*. I guess when you live in a glass cage you don't care a lot about aliens in the kitchen. When you're a woman alone in an apartment, aliens are pretty damn frightening. Except for Diesel. Diesel was inconvenient and confusing, and as much as I hate to admit it, Diesel was annoyingly likeable. Frightening had dropped low on the list. "So," I said to Rex, "why do you suppose I'm not afraid of Diesel? Probably some kind of alien magic, right?"

Rex was working at getting the cookie into his cheek pouch.

"And while we're having this discussion," I said to Rex, "I want to reassure you that I haven't forgotten about Christmas. I know it's only four days away, but I made cookies today. That's a good start, right?"

Truth is, there wasn't a trace of Christmas in my apartment. Counting down four days and

I didn't have a red bow or twinkle light in sight. Plus, I didn't have presents for anyone.

"How did this happen?" I asked Rex. "It seemed like just yesterday that Christmas was months away."

I OPENED MY eyes and shrieked. Diesel was standing beside my bed, staring down at me. I grabbed the sheet and pulled it up to my chin.

"What? How?" I asked.

He handed me a large-size take-out coffee. "Didn't we do this bit yesterday?"

"I thought you were gone."

"Yeah, but now I'm back. This is the part where you say, good morning, nice to see you, thanks for the coffee."

I pried the plastic lid off and examined the coffee. It looked like coffee. It smelled like coffee.

"Cripes," he said. "It's just coffee."

"A girl can never be too careful."

Diesel took the coffee back and drank it. "Rise and shine, gorgeous. We have things to do. We need to find Sandy Claws."

"I know why *I* need to find Sandy Claws. I don't know why *you* need to find Sandy Claws."

"Just being a good guy. I thought I'd come back and help you out."

Uh-hunh.

"Are you going to get up, or what?" he said.

"I'm not getting up with you standing there. And I'm not taking a shower with you in my apartment, either. Go out and wait for me in the hall."

He shook his head. "You are *so* untrusting."

"Go!"

I waited until I heard the front door open and close and then I slid out of bed and crept to the living room. Empty. I padded barefoot to the front door, opened the door, and looked out. Diesel was leaning against the opposite wall, arms crossed over his chest, looking bored.

"Just checking," I said. "You're not going to pop into my bathroom when I'm in there, are you?"

"No."

"Promise?"

"Honey, I don't need a thrill that bad."

I closed and locked the door, ran into the bathroom, took the fastest shower in the history of Plum, rushed back to my bedroom, and got dressed in my usual uniform of jeans, boots, and T-shirt. I refilled Rex's water bottle and gave him some hamster crunches, a raisin, and a corn chip for breakfast. He rushed out of his soup can, stuffed the raisin and the corn chip into his cheek pouch, and returned to his soup can.

I'd had a brilliant idea while I was in the shower. I knew a guy who might help me find Claws. His name was Randy Briggs. Briggs wasn't an elf, but he *was* only three feet tall. Maybe that was good enough.

I thumbed through my address book and found Briggs' phone number. Briggs was a self-employed computer geek. He usually worked at home. And he usually needed money.

"Hey," I said to him. "I have a job for you. I need an undercover elf."

"I'm not an elf."

"Yes, but you're short."

"Christ," Briggs said. And he hung up.

Probably best to talk to Briggs in person. Unfortunately, I now had a dilemma. I thought there was a possibility that Diesel might go away if I never opened the door and let him in. Problem was, I needed to go out.

I opened the door and looked at Diesel.

"Yeah, I'm still here," he said.

"I need to go someplace."

"No kidding."

"Alone."

"It's the supernatural thing, isn't it? It's still got you weirded out, right?"

"Um . . ."

He slung an arm around my shoulders. "I bet you think Spider-Man is a real cute guy. I bet you think it'd be fun to be friends with a guy like that."

"Maybe . . ."

"So just pretend I'm Spidey."

I looked at him sideways. "Are you Spidey?"

"No. He's a lot shorter."

I grabbed my bag and my keys and shrugged into my fleece-lined jacket. I locked my front door and took the stairs to the parking lot.

Diesel was right behind me. "We can take my car," he said.

"You have a car?"

There was a black Jaguar parked a few feet from the back entrance to my apartment building. Diesel beeped the Jag open with the remote.

"Wow," I said, "you do okay for an alien."

"I'm not an alien."

"Yeah, you keep saying that, but I don't know what else to call you."

"Call me Diesel."

I angled onto the passenger side seat and buckled in. "It's stolen, right?"

Diesel looked over at me and smiled.

Damn. "We're going to Cloverleaf Apartments on Grand. It's about a mile from here, off Hamilton."

The Cloverleaf apartment building looked a lot like mine. It was a big redbrick cube and strictly utilitarian. Three stories. A front and a back entrance. Parking lot in the rear.

Randy Briggs lived on the second floor. I'd met him a while back in a professional capacity. He'd been accused of carrying a concealed weapon and had failed to appear for a court appearance. I'd dragged him kicking and screaming back into the system. The charge had actually been borderline bogus, and Briggs was ultimately released without penalty.

"And why are we doing this?" Diesel asked, climbing the stairs to the second floor.

"There was a want ad in the paper for toy makers. When I called and inquired about Sandy Claws I got disconnected."

"And in your mind, this indicates that Claws is part of the toy maker operation."

"I think it's suspicious and warrants further investigation. I'm going to ask this guy I know to help infiltrate the operation."

"Is he a toy maker?"

"No. He has other talents."

We were in the stairwell and all of a sudden we were plunged into total darkness. I felt Diesel step closer, felt his hand protectively settle at my waist.

"Power blackout," I said. "Morelli told me they were happening all over Trenton."

"Great," Diesel said. "Just what I need. Power blackouts."

"Not a big deal," I told him. "Morelli said they last long enough to snarl traffic and then disappear."

"Sunshine, it's a bigger deal than you could possibly imagine."

I had no idea what he meant by that, but it didn't sound good. I was about to ask him when the lights popped back on, and we took the rest of the stairs to the second floor. I rapped on the door to 2B and there was no response. I put my ear to the door and listened.

"Hear anything?" Diesel asked.

"Television."

I rapped again. "Open the door, Randy. I know you're in there."

"Go away," Randy called. "I'm working."

"You're not working. You're watching television."

The door was wrenched open, and Randy glared out at me. "What?"

Diesel looked down at Randy. "You're a midget."

"No shit, Sherlock," Randy said. "And, just

for the record, midget is no longer politically correct."

"So, what do you like?" Diesel asked. "How about 'little dude'?"

Randy was holding a soup ladle, and he whacked Diesel in the knee with it. "Don't mess with me, wiseass."

Diesel reached down, grabbed Briggs by the front of his shirt, and lifted him three feet off the floor so they were eye level. "You need to get a sense of humor," Diesel said. "And you want to lose the soup ladle."

The soup ladle slid through Randy's fingers and clattered onto the parquet floor.

"So you don't want to be called a little dude," Diesel said. "What *do* you want to be called?"

"I'm a little *person*," Randy said, feet dangling in the air.

Diesel grinned at Randy. "Little person? That's the best you can do?"

Diesel set Randy back down on the floor, and Randy gave himself a shake, looking a lot like a bird settling its feathers.

"So," I said, "now that we have that straightened out . . ."

Briggs looked at me. "Here it comes."

"Have I ever asked for a favor?"

"Yes."

"Okay, but I saved your life."

"My life wouldn't have been in danger in the first place if it wasn't for you!"

"All I want is for you to pose as an elf."

Diesel gave a snort of laughter.

I cut my eyes to him, and he squelched the laughter down to a grin.

"I am *not* an elf," Briggs said. "Do I have pointy ears? No. Do I wear shoes that turn up on the ends? No. Do I enjoy this humiliation? No, no, no."

"I'll pay you for your time."

"Oh," Briggs said. "That's different."

I handed the ad over to Briggs. "All you have to do is answer this ad. Probably you don't even have to say you're an elf. Probably you could just tell him you're . . . qualified. And then when you go for the job interview, keep your eyes open for a guy named Sandy Claws. He's FTA."

"Give me a break. Santa Claus is FTA. How about the Easter Bunny? Is the Easter Bunny FTA, too?"

I flashed the photo of Sandy Claws at Briggs, and I spelled the name for him. I gave Briggs my card with my cell phone and pager number. And I left, not wanting to overstay my welcome, not wanting to give him time to change his mind.

I looked over at Diesel's knee when we were in the car. "Are you okay?"

"Yeah. He hits like a girl. Someone needs to show him how to swing a soup ladle."

THREE

CONNIE ROSOLLI MANAGES my cousin Vinnie's bail bonds office. Connie is a couple years older than me. She has big hair, big boobs, and a short fuse. And she could probably kick my butt from here to downtown Trenton. Good thing for me, Connie never feels compelled to kick my butt since Connie and I are friends.

I called Connie and asked her to check on water and electric accounts for Claws. Between semiclandestine computer searches and the tight-knit network of Burg women who love to dish, there isn't a lot of information Connie and I can't access.

I'd barely disconnected with Connie when my cell phone chirped.

It was my mother. "Help," she said.

I could hear a lot of hysterical shouting going on in the background. "What's happening?"

"Valerie took one of those home pregnancy tests, and now she's got herself locked in the bathroom."

"Don't worry about it. She'll come out when she gets hungry."

"It's our only bathroom! I've got two kids home from school for the holidays, an old lady with a bad bladder, and your father. Everybody needs to use the bathroom."

"And?"

"Do something! Shoot the lock off."

Now if I was any kind of a good sister and loving daughter I'd have sympathy for Valerie. I'd be worried about her physical and emotional health. The ugly truth is, Valerie was always the perfect child. And I was the kid who had the skinned knee, consistently flunked spelling, and lived in Lala Land. My entire childhood was an out-of-body experience. Even as adults, Valerie had the great marriage and gave birth to two grandchildren. I had the marriage from hell that ended before my father got the wedding reception paid off. So, I love my sister and wish her well, but it's hard not to smile once in a while now that her life is in the toilet.

"Uh-oh," Diesel said. "I'm not sure I like that smile."

"It sort of slipped out. Actually, I need you to help me with a domestic problem. I need a lock opened."

"Someday I should show you some of my other skills."

Oh boy. It's never good when a man starts talking about his skills. Before you know it you're in the garage watching a power tool demonstration. And after all the power tools are revved, there's only one tool left to haul out of the box. Someday a study should be done on the effect of testosterone production in the presence of a band saw.

Everyone was huddled outside the bathroom when I got to my parents' house. Mary Alice was galloping in circles and the rest of my family was alternately pacing and yelling and banging on the door.

"Pretty amazing," Diesel said to me. "I'm always knocked out by the way a family can be at the upper end of dysfunction and insanity and still work so well as a unit. Do you want me to open the door?"

"No." I was afraid they'd all rush in and someone would get trampled in the stampede. I went downstairs to the kitchen and out the back door. There was a small roof over the back stoop, and the roof butted up to the bathroom window. When I was a kid I used to sneak out the bathroom window to hang with my friends. "Give me a boost up," I said to Diesel. "I'll bring her out through the window. Then you can open the door."

Diesel laced his fingers together, I put my foot in his hands, and he lifted me to roof level. I scrambled onto the roof and glanced down at him. He was impressively strong.

"Could you stop a runaway freight train?" I asked.

"Probably not a freight train. That would be Superman."

I looked in the window at Valerie. She was sitting on the toilet lid, staring at the little test strip. She looked up when I knocked.

"Open up," I said. "It's cold out here."

She pressed her nose to the window and looked out. "Are you alone?"

"I'm with Diesel."

She looked down to the ground, and Diesel waved to her. It was a goofy little finger wave.

Valerie opened the window, and I climbed inside.

"What's going on?" I asked.

"Look at my test strip!"

"Maybe it made a mistake."

"It's the fifth time I've taken the test. They keep coming out positive. I'm pregnant. I'm goddamn pregnant. Albert Kloughn got me pregnant."

"Didn't you take precautions?"

"No, I didn't take precautions. Look at him! He looks like a loaf of yeast bread just before you bake it. He's soft and white and totally without substance. Who would have thought he'd have sperm? Do you know what this poor kid will look like?" Valerie wailed. "It'll look like a dinner roll."

"Maybe this isn't so bad. I thought you were all anxious to get married."

"I was anxious to get married, not to get pregnant. And I don't want to marry Kloughn. He lives with his *mother*, for God's sake. And he makes *no* money."

"He's a lawyer."

"He chases ambulances down the street. He might as well be a German shepherd."

It was true. Kloughn was having a difficult time getting his practice established and had resorted to listening to the police band.

"A woman has choices these days," I said.

"Not in this family!" Valerie was pacing and waving her arms. "We're Catholic, for cris-sake."

"Yeah, but you never go to church. It isn't like you have religion."

"You know what's left when the religion goes away? Guilt! Guilt *never* goes away. I'm stuck with the goddamn guilt for the rest of my life. And what about Mom? I even mention abortion, and she'll be crossing herself until her arm falls off."

"Don't tell her. Tell her the strip was negative."

Valerie stopped pacing and looked at me. "Would you get an abortion?"

Whoa. Me? I took a beat to think about it. "I don't know," I said. "I'm having a hard time relating. The closest I've come to childbirth is buying a hamster."

"Fine," Valerie said. "Suppose Rex was never born. Suppose the mommy hamster had an abortion and Rex was bagged up along with the dirty kennel bedding in the breeder hamster cage."

Sharp pain to the heart. "When you put it that way . . ."

"It's all his fault," Valerie said. "I'm going to find him. I'm going to track him down, and I'm going to maim him."

"Kloughn?"

"No. My dog turd ex-husband. If he hadn't run off with the babysitter this never would have happened. We were so happy. I don't know what went wrong. One minute we were a family and then next thing I know he's in the coat closet with the babysitter."

"Open up!" Grandma yelled from the other

side of the door. "I gotta go. Lock yourself in some other room."

"Just because you have the baby doesn't mean you have to marry Kloughn," I said. Although I actually thought Valerie could do a lot worse than Albert Kloughn. I liked Kloughn. He wasn't a big, handsome, super-cool guy, but he tried hard at everything, he was nice to Valerie and the girls, and there seemed to be genuine affection between them all. I wasn't sure anymore what made a good marriage. There had to be love, of course, but there were so many different kinds of love. And clearly, some love was more enduring than others. Valerie and I thought we'd found the loves of our lives, and look where that took us.

"Shoes," I said to Valerie. "When in doubt, I find it always helps if I buy a new pair of shoes. You should go shopping."

Valerie looked over at the door. "I could use a new pair of shoes, but I don't want to go out there."

"Use the window."

Valerie climbed out the window, got to the edge of the roof and hesitated. "This is scary."

"It's not a big deal," Diesel said. "Just hang your ass over the edge, and I'll bring you down."

Valerie looked back at me.

"Trust him," I said. Trust Superman, Spider-Man, E.T., the Ghost of Christmas Present . . . whoever the hell.

"I don't know," Valerie said. "This feels kind of high. I don't like the way this feels. Maybe I need to go back into the house." Valerie turned toward the window, and her foot slipped on the shingle roof. "Eeeeee," she shrieked, flailing out with her arms, grabbing me by my jacket. "Help! *Help!*"

She yanked me forward, and we both lost balance, slammed onto the roof, and rolled off the edge, clinging together. We crashed into Diesel, and the three of us went to the ground.

Diesel was flat on his back, I was on top of him, and Val was on top of me. The whole family came running out the back door and crowded around us.

"What's going on?" Grandma wanted to know. "Is this some new sex thing?"

"If she jumps on the pile, I'm out of here," Diesel said.

"Call 911!" my mother said. "Don't anybody move . . . your backs might be broken." She looked down at Valerie. "Can you wiggle your toes?"

"You didn't unlock the bathroom," my father said to Valerie. "Someone's gotta go back up and unlock the bathroom."

"Frank! I told you to call 911."

"We don't need 911," I said. "We just need for Valerie to get off me."

My mother pulled Valerie to her feet. "Is the baby okay? Did you hurt yourself? I can't believe you went out through the window."

"What about me?" I said. "I fell, too."

"You're always falling," my mother said. "You jumped off the garage roof when you were seven years old. And now people shoot at you." She shook her finger at me. "You're a bad influence on your sister. She never used to do things like this."

I was still lying on top of Diesel, and I was sort of enjoying it.

"I knew you'd come around," Diesel said to me.

I narrowed my eyes. "I have *not* come around."

My pager buzzed at my waist. I rolled off Diesel and checked the readout. It was Randy Briggs. I got to my feet and went into the house to use the phone while Diesel went upstairs to unlock the bathroom door.

My father followed Diesel to the bathroom. "Women," my father said. "There's gotta be a better way."

I was waiting at the door when Diesel came down. "Randy's got a job interview," I said.

"He's on the road. I have the address."

"What about the shopping?" Valerie asked.

"You have to shop by yourself," I said. "I have to find Sandy Claws. And why aren't you working?"

"I don't want to see Albert. I don't know what to say to him."

"I'm lost," Diesel said. "What's Albert got to do with working?"

"He's Valerie's boss."

"This is like watching daytime television," Diesel said.

"Look at you," my mother said to me. "It's almost Christmas and you're not wearing anything red." She took a Christmas tree pin off her shirt and attached it to my jacket. "Have you bought your tree yet?" she asked.

"I haven't had time to get a tree."

"You have to make time," my mother said. "Before you know it your life will be over and you'll be dead and then what?"

"You have a tree," I said. "Why can't I use yours?"

"Boy, you don't know much," my grandmother said.

Diesel was standing back on his heels, hands in his pockets, smiling, again.

"Go to the car," I said to Diesel. "And stop smiling."

"It's Christmastime," Diesel said. "Everybody smiles at Christmastime."

"Wait right here," my mother said. "Let me pack you a bag for lunch."

"No time," I said to my mother. "I need to get moving."

"It'll only take a minute!" She was already in the kitchen, and I could hear the refrigerator open and close and drawers open and close. And my mother returned with a bag of food.

"Thanks," I said.

Diesel looked in the bag and extracted a cookie. "Chocolate chip. My favorite."

I had a feeling *every* cookie was Diesel's favorite.

When we were both in the car, I turned to Diesel. "I want to know about you."

"There isn't a lot to tell. If I hadn't gotten dropped into your kitchen we wouldn't be having this conversation. If you met me on the street you'd think I was just another guy."

"So you're strong and can open locks. Anything else you're especially good at?"

Diesel smiled at me.

"All men think that," I said.

Diesel pulled onto Hamilton Avenue and turned left. "What happens when you find Claws?"

"I hand him over to the police. Then my

cousin Vinnie probably goes to the lockup and bails Claws out a second time."

"Why would Vinnie do that?"

"He gets paid more money. Claws has a local business, and he's signed his house over for security, so it's a good risk for Vinnie."

"And what if Claws doesn't want to be handed over to the police? Do you shoot him?"

"I hardly ever shoot people."

"This should be fun," Diesel said.

I cut my eyes to him. "Is there something you're not telling me?"

"Lots of things."

I put my finger to my lower lid.

"You have a problem?" he asked.

"Eye twitch."

"I bet that would go away if you got a Christmas tree."

"All right. Okay! I'll get a Christmas tree."

"When?"

"When I have time. And you're driving too slow. Where'd you learn how to drive, Florida?"

Diesel stopped the car in the middle of the road. "Take a deep breath."

"What are you doing? Are you nuts? You can't just stop in the middle of the road!"

"Take a deep breath. Count to ten."

I took a breath, and I counted to ten.

"Count slower," Diesel said.

The guy behind us honked his horn, and I cracked my knuckles. My eye was twitching like mad. "This isn't working," I said. "You're giving me heart palpitations. People in Jersey don't do *slow down*."

"We're sitting in traffic," Diesel said. "Notice that the car in front of us is less than a car length away and not moving. The only way to drive faster would be to drive on the sidewalk."

"What's your point?"

"I can't fit on the sidewalk."

"So do something supernatural," I said. "Can't you tip the car sideways or something? They do that in the movies all the time."

"Sorry, I flunked levitation."

My luck, I get a guy who flunked levitation.

Twenty minutes later, we parked across from a hole-in-the-wall storefront office. The makeshift sign in the window advertised IM- MEDIATE OPENINGS FOR MASTER TOY MAKERS. I wanted to take a closer look, so we left the car and crossed the street.

We stood on the sidewalk and looked through the dusty plate-glass window. Inside, the place was wall-to-wall little people.

"Are they elves?" I asked Diesel. "I don't see any pointy ears."

"Hard to tell at this distance, and I heard somewhere that elves don't necessarily have pointy ears."

"So elves could be walking around in our midst, disguised as normal, everyday, vertically challenged citizens."

Diesel looked at me and grimaced. "You don't really believe in elves, do you?"

"Of course not," I said. But the truth was that I didn't know *what* I believed in anymore. I mean, what the hell was Diesel? And if I believed in Diesel . . . why not believe in elves? "Do you see Briggs?" I asked him.

"He's at the back, talking to a big guy with a clipboard. And I don't see Claws."

We watched for a moment longer and then retreated to the Jag and worked our way through my mother's food bag. After a while Randy Briggs came out, walked halfway down the block, and got into the passenger side of a waiting car. The car pulled away, and we followed. Before we'd gone two blocks my cell phone buzzed in my bag.

"Cripes, is that you behind me in the Jag?" Briggs asked. "You bounty hunters must do okay to be riding around in a Jag."

"Diesel isn't a bounty hunter. He's an alien or something."

"Yeah, whatever. Man, I've never seen so

many little people in one place. It was like they came out of the woodwork. I thought I knew everyone in the area, but I didn't know *any* of these guys."

"Did you get hired?"

"Yeah, but I'm not going to make toys. I got a job in the office, setting up a Web site."

"What about Claws?"

"Didn't see him. No one said anything to me about anyone named Claws. I start work tomorrow. Maybe I'll see him at the factory."

"Factory?"

"Yeah, that's what this is . . . a small toy factory. They're going to make handmade toys and advertise that they were made by elves. Pretty cool, hunh?"

"Do you suppose some of these little people today actually were elves?"

There was a pause where I could imagine Briggs staring open-mouthed at the phone. "What are you, nuts?" he finally said.

"So, where is this factory?" I asked Briggs.

"It's in a light industrial complex off Route 1. You aren't going to screw up this job for me, are you? This is a dream job. The pay is good and the guy who hired me said the toilets are all made for little people. I won't have to climb up on a stool to take a crap."

"I'm not going to screw it up for you. What's the address?"

"I'm not telling you. I don't want to lose the job." And he hung up.

I looked over at Diesel. "When the car in front of us stops and Briggs gets out, I want you to run over him."

"I'd really like to do that, but then he'd probably be dead and we couldn't follow him to work tomorrow."

I glanced at the almost empty bag of food sitting between my feet, and I had an idea.

"What does Elaine do with all her cookies?" I asked Diesel.

"Is this a trick question?"

"She said she bakes cookies every day. Lots of cookies, if yesterday's batch was any indicator. So what does she do with them? They don't have family in the area. Sandy wasn't at home. Does she eat them all herself?"

"Maybe she gives them away."

"Turn around," I said. "Go back to the employment place."

It took less than five minutes for us to get back to the storefront office. "Wait here," I said. "I'll only be a minute." I jumped out of the car, ran across the street and into the office. It was still wall-to-wall little people but now the little people were all wearing fake elf ears. I was about ten feet into the fake elves when I realized the room had gone dead silent.

"Hi," I said brightly. "I saw the sign in the window, and I'd like to apply for a job."

"You're too big," someone said behind me. "These jobs are for elves."

"That's not fair," I said. "I could report you for height discrimination." I wasn't sure exactly who was in charge of height discrimination, but it seemed like there should be *some* agency *somewhere* that would address the issue. I mean, where are the protections for the masses? Where are the protections for people who are average?

"We don't want your kind here," someone else said. "Get out."

"My kind?"

"Big and stupid."

"Hey! Listen to me, shorty—"

A cookie came flying through the air and hit me in the back of the head. I looked down at the cookie. Gingerbread!

"Where'd this cookie come from?" I asked. "Do you have any more? Did Sandy's sister, Elaine, make this cookie?"

"Get her!" someone yelled, and I was hit with a barrage of cookies. They were coming from everywhere. Gingerbread, peanut butter, chocolate macaroons. The elves were berserk, yelling and swarming around me. I was hit in the forehead with an iced butter cookie, and someone bit me in the back of the leg. I had elves hanging on me like ticks on a dog.

I felt Diesel come up hard to my back. He wrapped his arm around me, holding me tight against him, and he hauled me out of there with my feet two inches off the ground. He was kicking elves out of the way as he went, occasionally grabbing one by the shirt and throwing him across the room. He got to the sidewalk, rammed the office door closed, and did his magical locking thing, trapping the elves inside.

Contorted little elf faces smushed up against the large glass windows, glaring out at us, yelling elf threats, their pudgy little elf middle fingers extended. Inside, the room was a wreck. Tables and chairs were overturned, and cookies were smashed everywhere.

Diesel set me on my feet, took me by the hand, and yanked me to the car. "What the hell was that about?" he asked. "I've never seen anything like it. A whole room filled with pissed-off little people. It was fucking frightening."

"I think they were elves. Did you see their ears?"

"Their ears were fake," Diesel said.

I slid onto the passenger seat and a sigh escaped. "I know. I just don't want to have to tell anyone I was attacked by a horde of angry little people. A horde of angry elves sounds better, somehow."

A fake elf smashed through the plate-glass door with a fire ax, and Diesel took off.

"Did you see the cookies?" I asked him. "They looked just like Elaine's cookies."

"Honey, all cookies look alike."

"Yes, but they *might* have been Elaine's cookies."

My cell phone chirped. "I'm at the mall," Valerie said, "and I need help. I can't remember everything that was on Mary Alice's list. I got her the Barbie, the television, the game, and the ice skates. I have the train and the computer at home. Do you remember what else she wanted?"

"How are you going to pay for all that?"

"MasterCard."

"It'll take you five years to pay it off."

"I don't care. It's Christmas. You have to do these things at Christmas."

Oh yeah. I kept forgetting. "Mary Alice had about fifty things on that list. The only one I remember is the pony."

"Omigod," Valerie cried. "The pony! How could I forget the pony?"

"Val, you can't get her a pony. This isn't *Little House on the Prairie*. We live in Trenton. Kids in Trenton don't get ponies."

"But she wants one. She'll hate me if I don't get her a pony. It'll ruin her Christmas."

Boy, I was really glad I had a hamster. I was planning on giving Rex a raisin for Christmas.

I hung up on Valerie, and I turned to Diesel. "Do you have any kids?"

"No."

"How do you feel about kids?"

"The same way I feel about fake elves. I think they're cute from a distance."

"Suppose you wanted to have kids . . . could you reproduce?"

Diesel looked over at me. "Could I reproduce? Yeah, I guess I could." He gave his head a shake. "I have to tell you, I am *never* again going to let anyone pop me in on someone. It's too weird. Not that this was my idea in the first place." He reached across me, into the bag my mother gave us, and found a leftover brownie. "Usually women are asking me to buy them a beer. Not you. You're asking me if I can reproduce."

"Make a turn at Clinton," I told him. "I want to have another chat with Elaine."

It was midafternoon and unusually gloomy when Diesel drove down Grape Street. Dark clouds swirled in the sky, and an eerie green light streaked through them. The air felt heavy and ominously charged. Doomsday air.

Lights were on in houses, and Elaine had her roof lights blazing, blinking out her season's greetings. Diesel parked in front of the house, and we both got out. The wind had picked up, and I pulled my chin in and walked head down to Sandy Claws' front porch.

"I'm very busy," Elaine said when she answered the door.

Diesel brushed past her, into the house. "It smells like you're still baking cookies."

Elaine followed Diesel into the kitchen, half running to keep up with Diesel's stride. "Pecan shortbread for tomorrow," she said. "And big cookies with M&Ms in them."

"I'm curious," Diesel said. "Who eats all these cookies?"

"The elves, of course."

Diesel and I exchanged glances.

"They're not really elves," Elaine said. "Sandy just likes to call them that. His little elves. Sandy is so clever. He has a whole scheme worked out to sell toys. It's because of his name, Sandy Claws. Have you noticed how it sounds like Santa Claus?"

"How many elves are you feeding?" Diesel asked Elaine.

"Goodness, I don't know, but there must be a lot of them. I make dozens of cookies every day."

"And they go where?"

"I don't know, exactly. Lester stops around and picks them up. Lester is Sandy's production manager."

"About five-foot-ten? Gray hair, slim, dark-rimmed glasses?" Diesel asked.

"Yes. That's him," Elaine said.

The guy who was interviewing elves.

"I don't mean to be rude," Elaine said, "but you're going to have to leave now. I have to finish my baking."

"You don't mind if I look around, do you?" Diesel asked.

Elaine nervously picked at her apron. "I don't see why you would want to do that. Sandy isn't here."

Diesel opened the door to a small downstairs powder room and looked inside. "Are you sure you don't know where Sandy is?"

"Stop that!" Elaine said. "Stop snooping in my house. I'm going to call the police."

"We have a legal right to search this house," Diesel said. "Isn't that right, Steph?"

"Yep. We received that right when your brother signed his bond agreement."

"This whole thing is so silly," Elaine said. "All over a couple power tools and some paint. And Sandy wouldn't have had to steal anything if the store had been open. You can't stop a whole production line just because you run out of Morning Glory paint. And everyone knows elves work at night. My goodness, Sandy has enough labor problems without having a whole crew sit out until the stores open at nine A.M."

"I thought they weren't actually elves."

"Real elves, fake elves . . . what's the difference? They all get time and a half after five o'clock."

Diesel leaned against the kitchen counter, arms crossed over his chest. "When was the last time you talked to Sandy?"

"He called me at lunchtime." Elaine pressed her lips together.

"Did you tell him I was looking for him?"

"Yes." Elaine glanced at me and then looked back at Diesel. "I've been trying to be discreet in front of Ms. Plum."

"Too late for that," Diesel said. "I was dropped into her kitchen."

Elaine looked horrified. "How did that happen?"

Diesel did a palms up and an *I don't know* shrug. "It would have to be a team effort. I'm not easy to move."

Elaine wiped her hands on her apron. "I'm sorry, but Sandy doesn't want to talk to you. He wants to be left alone."

"I'm curious," Diesel said. "Why the name Sandy Claws?"

Elaine took a tray of cookies from the oven and set them on top of the stove. "His birth name was Sandor Clausen. We thought it was appropriate that he return to his birth name now that he's retired. Sandy Claws seemed like a natural derivative."

"Sandor Clausen," Diesel said. "I didn't read that far back in the file."

Hold on here. File? What the heck are they talking about? Okay, now I'm really confused. Clearly, Elaine and Diesel know each other. It sounds like they recognized each other from the very beginning, and Diesel kept that tidbit of information secret from me. This was presenting me with the opportunity to practice some anger management.

"Sandor wants to make toys. He should be able to do what he wants in retirement," Elaine said.

"No one cares if he makes toys in his retirement," Diesel said. "I'm here because Ring followed him out."

The surprise was obvious. "Ring!"

Diesel pushed off the counter, took a cookie, and turned to leave. "You have to persuade Sandor to cooperate with me," he said to Elaine. "I'm trying to protect him."

Elaine nodded. "I didn't know about Ring."

Ring? Am I understanding this correctly? There's someone or some*thing* named Ring involved in this mess?

I didn't say a word until we were back in the Jag. I was trying to look casual, but I was fuming inside. I felt like demon Stephanie with glowing red eyeballs and snarling gargoyle mouth. Fortunately, the image was all internal. Or at least I *hoped* it was all internal. "What the hell was that all about?" I asked Diesel, making an effort to squelch the demon thing, going with steely eyes and tight lips, instead.

Diesel turned in his seat and looked at me. Thinking. Making silent assessments.

"Trying to decide what to tell me?" I asked, still sticking with the steely eyes.

"Yeah." He was Mr. Serious. Not smiling.

I waited him out.

"Some human beings have the ability to operate beyond what are considered to be normal limitations," Diesel finally said. "Most of these people tend to have rogue personalities and work pretty much alone, playing by their own rules. Sandor was one of the best. Very powerful and very good. Unfortunately, he's old, and he's lost his power. So he's retired. Usually retirees go into an assisted living complex in Lakewood. Sandor tried it and decided he wanted out."

"And Ring?"

"Ring's a bad guy. Old, like Sandor. The story I was told is that Ring and Sandor were best friends when they were kids. I guess they both knew they were different, and this was a secret they shared. As they got older the differences in their personalities drove a wedge between them. Ring was using his power to dominate people and to amuse himself. And Sandor was using his power mostly to clean up after Ring. When they reached full power in their early twenties, some of Ring's peers got together and Ring was told to stop all superpower activity.

"Ring refused to stop, of course. Ring loved causing chaos. And Ring was drunk on his own power. Unfortunately, Ring was so powerful and so clever, there were only a few people who could control him. And it was virtually impossible to contain him.

"Sandor was one of the few who had matching power. Much of Sandor's life was spent battling Ring, trying to eliminate him."

"Eliminate?"

Diesel did a slash across the throat and a looking-dead face. "Anyway, Sandor never succeeded, but he did manage to cripple Ring from time to time, making Ring ineffective for years or months, sending Ring into hiding."

"And now Ring's lost his power, too?"

"Pretty much. He was in the locked ward at Lakewood. They have a special area for villains and Alzheimer's. Somehow, he managed to get out. I guess he has power left that no one knew about."

So here I am having a conversation about what? Superheroes! And I'm having it with the guy who rolled his eyes because I suggested the possible reality of elves.

"Where do you fit into this?" I asked.

"I'm kind of like you. I track people down who've strayed from the system. And I go after bad guys."

FOUR

Okay. I'm sitting in a car with a guy who thinks he's part of a supersociety. And the weird thing is . . . I'm half believing him. Truth is, I kind of like the idea that there are some superheroes out there, trying to save us from ourselves. I'm not sure how I feel about Diesel being one of them.

"Let me get this straight," I said to Diesel. "You're after Ring, right? You want to get him back to Lakewood. And in the meantime, you're worried Sandor is in danger."

Diesel pulled away from the curb, cruised down the street, and turned at the corner. "When Ring was in his prime he worked with electricity."

"What, like with PSE&G?"

That cracked Diesel up. "No. Like he was Electrical Man. He could make lightning. I don't know how he did it. I always thought it was kind of show-off, but hell, he could do a lot of damage. I don't know how dangerous he is now. I have a feeling he tried to destroy the toy store but only could get up enough juice to knock boxes off the shelves. And then I'm guessing he got pissed off and tore the sign off the front of the store. A few of the boxes in the store were singed, so it seemed like he was able to throw some electricity, but maybe not accurately and probably of short duration. Nothing to lose sleep over. The power outages are different. If he's responsible for the power outages it means he's gaining power somehow. And I don't like the way the air feels around Sandor's house."

"Do you think Sandor will get in touch with you?" I asked Diesel.

"No. He's always worked alone. I can't see him asking for help now."

My phone buzzed in my handbag.

"You were right about the horse," Valerie said. "I don't know what I was thinking. It's impossible to get a horse at this late date. It isn't like they sell them in Sears. So I got Mary Alice a book about horses, and I got her a sleeping bag with horses on it. I have to get something for Mom now. Do you have any ideas?"

"I thought you got Mom a robe."

"Yes, but that doesn't seem like enough. It's only one box to open. What do you think about perfume? Or a blouse? And I can get a night-gown to go with the robe. And then some slippers."

"Maybe you've shopped enough for one day, Val. Maybe you're sort of . . . carried away with shopping."

"I can't stop now. I hardly have anything! And there are only three shopping days left."

"How much coffee have you had today, Val? You might want to think about cutting back on the coffee."

"Gotta go," Valerie said. And she disconnected.

"So, where were we?" I asked Diesel.

"We were saving the world."

"Oh yeah." Personally, I'd be happy just to collect my finder's fee on Sandy Claws so I could make the minimum payment on my credit card.

"Do you think Connie has the water and electric information on Claws yet?"

I called Connie, but the information wasn't helpful. No additional accounts for Sandy Claws. I had her try Sandor Clausen. Big zero there, too.

Diesel stopped for a light, and I saw his eyes

cut to the rearview mirror and the line of his mouth tighten. "I'm getting a real bad feeling."

Diesel made a U-turn and suddenly there was a flash of light in the sky in front of us. The light was followed by a low rumbling, and then there was another flash and smoke billowed over the rooftops.

Diesel stared at the smoke. "Ring."

It took us less than a minute to return to Claws' house. Diesel parked the Jag, and we joined the small group of people who'd collected in the street, eyes wide, mouths open in astonishment. Not often you see lightning at this time of the year. Not often you see the sort of carnage that resulted from the strike.

The Claws house was perfectly intact, but the life-size plastic Santa that had been strapped to the next-door neighbors' chimney had been blasted off the roof and lay in a smoking, melted red blob on the sidewalk. And the neighbors' garage was on fire.

"He melted Santa," I said to Diesel. "This is serious stuff."

Diesel gave his head a disbelieving shake. "He hit the wrong house. All those years of inciting terror and this is what it comes down to—frying some molded plastic. And not even the *right* molded plastic."

"I saw the whole thing," a woman said. "I

was on the porch, checking my lights, and a ball of fire swooped out of the sky and hit the Patersons' garage. And then a second ball came in and knocked the Santa Claus off the roof. I've never seen anything like it. Santa just flew off the roof!"

"Did anyone else see the fireballs?" Diesel asked.

"There was a man on the sidewalk, across the street from Sandy and Elaine's house, but he's gone now. He was an older gentleman, and he seemed pretty upset."

A police car arrived, lights flashing. A fire truck followed close behind and hoses were run to the garage.

Elaine was on her porch. She had a heavy wool coat pulled around her dumpling body, and she had a belligerent set to her mouth.

Diesel draped an arm across my shoulders. "Okay, partner, let's talk to Elaine."

Elaine drew the jacket tighter when we got closer. "Crazy old fool," she said. "Doesn't know when to stop."

"Did you see him?" Diesel asked.

"No. I heard the crackle of electricity, and I knew he was out there. By the time I got to the porch, he was gone. It's just like him to attack at Christmas, too. The man is pure evil."

"It's not a good idea for you to stay here,"

Diesel said. "Do you have someplace else to go? Would you like me to find a safe house for you?"

Elaine tipped her chin up a fraction of an inch. "I'm not leaving my home. I have cookies to make. And someone has to keep the bird feeders filled in the backyard. The birds count on it. I've been taking care of Sandor ever since my husband died, fifteen years ago, and I've never once had to resort to a safe house."

"Sandor was always able to protect you. Now that his power is failing you need to be more careful," Diesel said.

Elaine bit her lower lip. "You'll have to excuse me. I have to get back to my baking."

Elaine retreated into her house, and Diesel and I were left on the porch. The garage fire was almost extinguished, and someone, who I suspected was Mrs. Paterson, was attempting to pry Santa off the sidewalk with a barbecue spatula.

My phone chirped from my bag.

"If that's your sister again, I'm throwing your phone in the river," Diesel said.

I pulled the phone out of my bag and pressed the off button. I *knew* it was my sister. And there was an outside chance Diesel was serious about throwing the phone in the river.

"Now what?" I asked Diesel.

"Lester knows where the factory is."

"Forget it. I'm not going back to the employment office."

Diesel smiled down at me. "What's the matter? Is the big bad bounty hunter afraid of the little people?"

"Those fake elves were crazy. And they were mean!"

Diesel ruffled my hair. "Don't worry. I won't let them be mean to you."

Swell.

DIESEL PARKED HALF a block from the employment office and we sat wordlessly staring at the emergency vehicles in front of us. A fire truck, an EMT truck, and four police cars. The windows and the front door to the office were shattered, and a charred chair had been dragged out to the sidewalk.

We left the car and walked over to a couple cops I recognized. Carl Costanza and Big Dog. They were standing back on their heels, hands resting on their utility belts, surveying the damage with the sort of enthusiasm usually reserved for watching grass grow.

"What happened?" I asked.

"Fire. Riot. The usual. It's pretty ugly in there," Carl said.

"Bodies?"

"Cookies. Smashed cookies all over the place."

Big Dog had an elf ear in his hand. He held it up and looked at it. "And these things."

"It's an elf ear," I said.

"Yeah. These ears are all that's left of the little buggers."

"Did they burn?" I asked.

"No. They ran," Carl said. "Who would have thought the little guys could run that fast? Couldn't catch a single one of them. We arrived on the scene, and they took off like roaches when the light goes on."

"How did the fire get started?"

Carl shrugged and looked up at Diesel. "Who's he?"

"Diesel."

"Does Joe know about him?"

"Diesel is from out of town." Way out. "We're working a skip together."

There wasn't anything more to be learned from the employment office, so we left Carl and Big Dog and returned to the car. The sun was shining some place other than Trenton. Streetlights were on. And the temperature had dropped by ten degrees. My feet were wet from slogging through two fire scenes and my nose was numb, frozen like a popsicle.

"Take me home," I said to Diesel. "I'm done."

"What? No shopping? No Christmas cheer? Are you going to let your sister beat you out in the present race?"

"I'll shop tomorrow. I swear I will."

DIESEL PARKED THE Jag in my apartment building parking lot and got out of the car.

"It's not necessary to see me to the door," I said. "I imagine you want to get back to the Ring search."

"Nope. I'm done for the day. I thought we'd have something to eat and then chill in front of the TV."

I was momentarily speechless. That wasn't the evening I had planned out in my mind. I was going to stand in a scalding hot shower until I was all wrinkly. Then I was going to make myself a peanut butter and Marshmallow Fluff sandwich. I like peanut butter and Fluff because it combines the main course with the dessert and it doesn't involve pots. Maybe I'd watch some television after dinner. And if I was lucky I'd be watching it with Morelli.

"That sounds great," I said, "but I have plans for tonight. Maybe some other time."

"What are your plans?"

"I'm seeing Morelli."

"Are you sure?"

"Yes." No. I wasn't sure. I figured the possibility was about fifty percent. "And I wanted to take a shower."

"Hey, you can take a shower while I make dinner."

"You can cook?"

"No," he said. "I can dial."

"Okay, so here's the thing, I don't feel entirely comfortable with you in my apartment."

"I thought you were getting used to the Super Diesel thing."

Old Mr. Feinstein shuffled past us on his way to his car. "Hey, chicky," he said to me. "How's it going? You need any help here? This guy looks shifty."

"I'm fine," I told Mr. Feinstein. "Thanks for the offer, though."

"See that," I said to Diesel. "You look shifty."

"I'm a pussycat," Diesel said. "I haven't even come on to you. Okay, maybe a little teasing, but nothing serious. I haven't grabbed you . . . like this." He wrapped his fingers around my jacket lapels and pulled me to him. "And I haven't kissed you . . . like this." And he kissed me.

My toes curled in my shoes. And heat

slashed through my stomach and headed south.

Damn.

He broke from the kiss and smiled down at me. "It isn't as if I've done anything like that, right?"

I gave him a two-handed shot to the chest, but he didn't budge, so I took a step back. "There will be no kissing, no fooling around, no *anything*."

"Sure."

I did an *I give up* gesture, turned, and went into the building. Diesel followed after me, and we waited in silence for the elevator. The doors opened, and Mrs. Bestler smiled out at me. Mrs. Bestler is just about the oldest person I've ever seen. She lives alone on the third floor, and she likes to play elevator operator when she gets bored.

"Going up," she called out.

"Second floor," I said.

The elevator doors closed, and Mrs. Bestler chanted, "Ladies' handbags, Santa's workshop, better dresses." She looked at me and shook her finger. "Only three shopping days left."

"I know. I know!" I said. "I'll go shopping tomorrow. I swear, I will."

Diesel and I stepped out of the elevator, and Mrs. Bestler sang, "*It's beginning to look a lot like*

Christmas," as we walked down the hall.

"I'm laying odds she's eighty proof," Diesel said, opening my door.

My apartment was dark, lit only by the blue digital clock on my microwave and the single, red, blinking diode on my answering machine.

Rex ran on his wheel in the kitchen. The soft whir of his wheel reassured me that Rex was safe and probably there weren't any bridge trolls hiding in my closet tonight. I flipped the light, and Rex immediately stopped running and blinked out at me. I dropped a couple Froot Loops into his cage from the box on the counter, and Rex was a happy camper.

I hit the play button on the answering machine and unbuttoned my jacket.

First message. "It's Joe. Give me a call."

Next message. "Stephanie? It's your mother. You don't have your cell phone on. Is something wrong? Where are you?"

Third message. "It's Joe again. I'm stuck on this job, and I won't make it over tonight. And don't call me. I can't always talk. I'll call back when I can."

Fourth message. "Christ," Morelli said.

"Guess it's just you and me," Diesel said, grinning. "Good thing I'm here. You'd be lonely."

And the terrible part was that he was right.

I had one foot on the slippery slope of Christmas depression. Christmas was sliding away from me. Five days, four days, three days . . . and before my eyes, Christmas would come and go without me. And I'd have to wait an entire year to take another crack at a ribbons and bows, candy canes, and eggnog Christmas.

"Christmas isn't ribbons and bows and presents," I said to Diesel. "Christmas is about good will, right?"

"Wrong. Christmas is about presents. And Christmas trees. And office parties. Boy, you don't know much, do you?"

"Do you really believe that?"

"Aside from all the religious blah, blah, blah, which we won't get into . . . I think Christmas is whatever turns you on. That's what I really believe. Everyone decides what they want out of Christmas. Then everyone gets a shot at making it happen."

"Suppose every year you blow it? Suppose every year you screw up Christmas?"

He crooked his arm around my neck. "Are you screwing up Christmas, kiddo?"

"I can't seem to get to it."

Diesel looked around. "I noticed. No garlands of green shit. No angels, no Rudolphs, no kerplunkers or tartoofers."

"I used to have some tartoofers but my

apartment got firebombed and they all went up in smoke."

Diesel shook his head. "Don't you hate when that happens?"

I WOKE UP in a sweat. I was having a nightmare. There were only two days left until Christmas, and I still hadn't bought a single present. I gave myself a mental head smack. It wasn't a nightmare. It was true. Two days until Christmas.

I jumped out of bed and scurried into the bathroom. I took a fast shower and power-dried my hair. Yikes. I tamed it with some gel, got dressed in my usual jeans, boots, and T-shirt, and went to the kitchen.

Diesel lounged against the sink, coffee cup in hand. There was a white bakery bag on the counter, and Rex was awake in his cage, leisurely working his way to the heart of a jelly doughnut.

"Morning, sunshine," Diesel said.

"There are only two days left until Christmas," I said. "Two days! And I wish you would stop letting yourself into my apartment."

"Yeah, right, that's gonna happen. Have you given Santa your list? Have you been naughty?"

It was early in the morning for an eye roll, but I managed one anyway. I poured myself coffee and took a doughnut.

"It was nice of you to bring doughnuts," I said. "But Rex will get a cavity in his fang if he eats that whole thing."

"We're making progress," Diesel said. "You didn't shriek when you saw me here. And you didn't check the coffee and doughnuts for alien poison."

I looked down at the coffee and had a rush of panic. "I wasn't thinking," I said.

Half an hour later we were on a side street with a good view of Briggs' apartment building. Briggs was going to work today. And we were going to follow him. He'd lead us to the toy factory, I'd locate Sandy Claws, I'd snap the cuffs on him, and *then* I could have Christmas.

At exactly eight-fifteen, Randy Briggs strutted out of his building and got into a specially equipped car. He cranked the engine over and drove out of the lot, heading for Route 1. We followed a couple cars back, keeping Briggs in sight.

"Okay," I said to Diesel. "You flunked levitation and obviously you can't do the lightning thing. What's your specialty? What tools have you got on your utility belt?"

"I told you, I'm good at finding people. I have heightened sensory perception." He cut his eyes to me. "Bet you didn't think I knew big words like that."

"Anything else? Can you fly?"

Diesel blew out a sigh. "No. I can't fly."

Briggs stayed on Route 1 for a little over a mile and then exited. He left-turned at the corner and entered a light industrial complex. He drove past three businesses before pulling into a parking lot, adjacent to a one-story redbrick building that was maybe five thousand square feet. There were no signs announcing the name or the nature of the business. A toy soldier on the door was the only ornamentation.

We gave Briggs a half hour to get into the building and settle himself. Then we crossed the lot and pushed through the double glass doors, into the small reception area. The walls were brightly colored in yellow and blue. There were several chairs lined up against one wall. Half the chairs were big and half were small. The boundary to the reception area was set by a desk. Behind the desk were a couple cubbies. Briggs was sitting in one of them.

The woman behind the desk looked at Diesel and me and smiled. "Can I help you?"

"We're looking for Sandy Claws," Diesel said.

"Mr. Claws isn't in this morning," the woman said. "Perhaps I can help you."

Briggs' head snapped up at the sound of Diesel's voice. He looked over at us and worry lines creased his high forehead.

"Do you expect him in later today?" I asked.

"It's hard to say. He keeps his own schedule."

We left the building, and I called and asked for Briggs.

"Don't call me here," Briggs said. "This is a great job. I don't want it screwed up. And I'm not going to inform for you, either." And he hung up.

"I guess we could stake out the building," I said to Diesel. I wanted to do this just behind poke out my eye with a burning stick.

Diesel pushed his seat back and stretched his legs. "I'm beat," he said. "I worked the night shift. How about if you take the first watch."

"The night shift?"

"Sandor and Ring have a long history in Trenton. I made the rounds of some of Ring's old haunts after I left you last night, but I didn't turn anything up."

He crossed his arms over his chest and almost instantly seemed to be asleep. At ten-thirty my cell phone rang.

"Hey, girlfriend," Lula said. "What's up?"

Lula does filing for the bonds office. She was a ho' in a previous life but has since amended her ways. Her wardrobe has pretty much stayed the same. Lula's a big woman who likes the challenge of buying clothes that are two sizes too small.

"Not much is up," I said. "What's up with you?"

"I'm going shopping. Two days to Christmas and I don't have nothing. I'm heading for Quakerbridge Mall. You want to ride shotgun?"

"*Yes!*"

LULA CHECKED HER rearview mirror for one last look at Diesel before leaving the toy factory parking lot. "That man is *fine*. I don't know where you find these guys, but it isn't fair. You got the market cornered on *hot*."

"He's actually a superhero, sort of."

"Don't I know it. I bet he got superhero *boys*, too."

Lula was sounding a lot like Grandma. I didn't want to think about Diesel's *boys*, so I put the radio on. "I have to be back to relieve him at three o'clock," I said.

"Dang," Lula said, pulling into Quakerbridge. "Look here at this parking lot. It's full.

This mother is *full*. Where am I supposed to park? I only got two days to shop. I can't deal with this parking thing. And what's with all the best spots going to the handicapped? You see any handicap cars in all these handicap places? How many handicap people they think we got in Jersey?"

Lula rode around the lot for twenty minutes, but she didn't find a parking space. "Look at this itty bitty Sentra nosed up to a wreck of a Pinto," Lula said, wheeling around so she had the front bumper of her Firebird inches from the back bumper of the Sentra. "Uh-oh," she said, easing forward, "look how that Sentra's moving forward all by itself. Before you know it, there's gonna be a parking space available on account of that Pinto is rolling into the driving lane."

"You can't just push a car out of its space!" I said.

"Sure I can," Lula said. "See? I already did it." Lula had her handbag over her shoulder, and she was out of the Firebird, booking toward the mall entrance. "I got a lot to do," Lula said. "I'll meet you back at the car at two-thirty."

I GLANCED DOWN at my watch. It was two-thirty. And I only had one present. I'd gotten a pair of gloves for my dad. That was a no-brainer. I got him gloves every year. He counted on it. I was at a loss for everyone else. I'd given Valerie all my good gift ideas. And the mall was a mob scene. Too many shoppers. Not enough clerks at registers. Picked-over merchandise. Why did I let this go to the last minute? Why do I go through this *every* year? Next year I'm getting my Christmas presents in July. I swear, I am.

Lula and I reached the car simultaneously. I had my little bag with the gloves, and Lula had four huge shopping bags filled to bursting.

"Wow," I said, "you're good. I only got gloves."

"Hell, I don't even know what's in these bags," Lula said. "I just started grabbing stuff that was close to a register. I figure I'll sort it out later. Everybody always takes their shit back anyway, so it don't really matter what you buy the first time around."

Lula cruised toward the exit and her eyes lit when she came to the edge of the lot. "Do you believe this?" she said. "They set up a Christmas tree lot here. I *need* a Christmas tree. I'm gonna stop. I'll only be a minute. I'm gonna get myself a Christmas tree."

Fifteen minutes later we had two six-foot Christmas trees stuffed into Lula's four-foot trunk. One tree for Lula. And one tree for me. We secured the trunk lid with a bungee cord, and we were on our way.

"Good thing we saw that tree lot so you could get a tree, too," Lula said. "You can't have Christmas without a Christmas tree. Boy, I *love* Christmas."

Lula was dressed in knee-high, white fake-fur boots that made her look like Sasquatch. She had her bottom half stuffed into skin-tight red spandex pants that magically had gold glitter embedded in them. She was wearing a red sweater with a green felt Christmas tree appliqué. And she had it topped off with a yellow-dyed rabbit-fur jacket. Every time Lula moved, yellow rabbit hairs escaped from the jacket and floated on the air like dandelion fluff. Behind us, the tree lot was lost in a yellow haze.

"Okay," Lula said, stopping for a light. "We got Christmas knocked. We're on our way to Christmas." The light turned and the guy in front of us hesitated. Lula leaned on the horn and gave him the finger. "Move it," she yelled. "You think we got all day? It's Christmas, for chrissake. We got things to do." She reached the highway and took off, ripping into "Jingle Bells" at the top of her lungs. "*Jingle bells, jingle bells, jingle all the wa-a-a-ay,*" she sang.

I put my finger to my eye.

"Hey, you got that eye twitch again?" she asked. "You should do something about that eye twitch. You should see a doctor."

Lula was on the third chorus of "Silent Night" when she parked next to the black Jag. I got out of the Firebird and bent to talk to Diesel.

"Lula and I can take the next watch," I told him. "If anything happens, I'll call you."

"Sounds good," Diesel said. "I could use a break. It's been quiet all day, and that's the way I like it. If there aren't any more disturbances, Sandor will eventually come back to his workshop."

"Don't you worry, Diesel honey," Lula said from behind me. "We'll watch the heck out of this place. *Peace and Quiet*'s my middle name."

Diesel checked Lula out and smiled.

"So what's the deal?" Lula wanted to know when Diesel left.

"I'm after an FTA named Sandy Claws. He owns this toy factory."

"And what's with the car next to us? It's got a big booster seat behind the wheel. And what are those levers on the steering column?"

"Most of the employees here are little people."

Sometimes when Lula got excited her eyes opened wide and popped out like big white duck eggs. This was one of those duck-egg-eye times. "Are you shitting me? Midgets? A whole building full of midgets? I love midgets. I've had this thing for midgets ever since I saw *The Wizard of Oz*. Except for that guy, Randy Briggs. He was a nasty little bugger."

"Briggs is here, too," I said. "He's working in the office."

"Hunh. I wouldn't mind kicking his ass."

"No ass kicking!"

Lula stuck her lower lip out and pulled her eyes back into their sockets. "I know that. You think I don't know that? I got a sense of decorum. Hell, *Decorum*'s my middle name."

"Anyway, you won't see him," I said, "because we're just going to sit here."

"I don't want to sit here," Lula said. "I want to see the midgets."

"They're little people now. Midget is politically incorrect."

"Cripes, I can't keep up on this political correct shit. I don't even know what to call *myself*. One minute I'm black. Then I'm African American. Then I'm a person of color. Who the hell makes these rules up, anyhow?"

"Well, whoever they are, little people, elves, or whatever, you'll see them when the shift changes, and they go home."

"How do you know this Claws guy didn't

come in through a back door? I bet this factory's got a big ol' back door. It's probably got a loading dock. I think we should go ask if Claws has come in yet."

Lula had a point. There was for sure a back door.

"All right," I said, "I guess it won't do any harm to try the woman at the desk one more time."

Briggs went pale when we entered the reception area. And the woman at the desk looked apologetic. "I'm afraid he's still not here," she said to me.

"Where are the toys made?" Lula asked, walking toward the door to the factory. "I bet they're made in here. Boy, I'd really like to see the toys getting made."

The woman behind the desk was on her feet. "Mr. Claws prefers not to have visitors in the workshop."

"I'll just take a quick peek," Lula said. And she opened the door. "Holy cats," she said, walking into the warehouse. "Will you look at this! It's a bunch of freaking elves."

Briggs rounded the reception desk, and we both ran after Lula.

"They're not really elves," Briggs said, skidding to a stop in front of her.

Lula was hands on hips. "The hell they

aren't! I guess I know an elf when I see one. Look at those ears. They all got elf ears."

"They're fake ears, stupid," Briggs said to Lula. "It's a marketing ploy."

"Don't go calling me stupid," Lula said to Briggs.

"Stupid, stupid, stupid," Briggs said.

"Listen up, you moron," Lula said. "I could squash you like a bug if I wanted. You gotta be more careful who you disrespect."

"It's her," one of the elves yelled, pointing his finger at me. "She's the one who started the fire in the employment office."

"Fire?" Lula asked. "What's he talking about?"

"She started the riot," someone else yelled. "Get her!"

The elves all jumped up from their work stations and rushed at me on their little elf legs.

"Get her. Get her!" they were all yelling. "Get the big stupid troublemaker."

"Hey!" Lula said. "Hold on here. What the—"

I grabbed Lula by the back of her jacket and yanked her toward the door. "Run! And don't look back."

FIVE

WE BARRELED THROUGH the workroom door to the reception area, pushed through the front door, sprinted across the lot and jumped into the car. Lula popped the doors locked, and the elves swarmed around us.

"These aren't elves," Lula said. "I know elves. Elves are cute. These are evil gremlins. Look at their pointy teeth. Look at their red, glowing eyes."

"I don't know about gremlins," I said. "I think the guy with the red eyes is just a little person with bad teeth and a hangover."

"Hey, what's that noise? What are they doing to the back of my Firebird?"

We turned and looked out the back window, and we were horrified to find that the elves had dragged the trees out of the trunk.

"That's my Christmas tree!" Lula yelled. "Get away. Leave that tree alone."

No one was listening to Lula. The elves were in a frenzy, tearing the trees limb from limb, jumping up and down on the branches.

Suddenly there was an elf on the hood. And then a second elf scrambled up after the first.

"Holy crap," Lula said. "This here's a horror movie." She shoved the key into the ignition, put her foot to the floor, and rocketed across the lot. One elf flew off instantly. The second elf had his hands wrapped around the windshield wipers, his snarling face pressed to the windshield. Lula made a fast right turn, one of the windshield wipers snapped, and the elf sailed away like a Frisbee, windshield wiper still clutched in his little elf hand.

"Fuck youuuuuuuu," the elf sang as he sailed away.

We went a mile down Route 1 before either of us said a word.

"I don't know what those nasty-assed little things were," Lula finally said. "But they need to learn some people skills."

"That was sort of embarrassing," I said.

"Fuckin' A."

And I still didn't have a Christmas tree.

It was a little after five when I waved good-bye to Lula and trudged into my building. My apartment was quiet. No Diesel. I said a silent *thank goodness*, but the truth is, I was disappointed. I hung my jacket on a hook in the hall and listened to my messages.

"Stephanie? It's your mother. Mrs. Krienski said she didn't get a Christmas card from you. You *did* mail them, didn't you? And, I'm making a nice pot roast for supper tonight if you want to come over. And your father got a tree for you at the service station. They were having a close-out sale. He said he got a good deal."

Omigod. A close-out tree from the service station. Does it get any worse than that?

MARY ALICE AND Angie were in front of the television when I got to my parents' house. My father was sleeping in his chair. My sister was upstairs, throwing up. And my mom and grandmother were in the kitchen.

"I didn't misplace them," Grandma said to my mother. "Someone *took* them."

"Who would take them?" my mother asked. "That's ridiculous."

I knew I was going to regret asking, but I couldn't help myself. "What's missing?"

"My teeth," Grandma said. "Someone took my teeth. I had them setting out in a glass with one of them whitening tablets and next thing they were gone."

"How was your day?" my mother asked me.

"Average. Got attacked for the second time by a horde of angry elves, but aside from that it was okay."

"That's nice," my mother said. "Could you stir the gravy?"

Valerie came in and clapped a hand over her mouth at the sight of the pot roast, sitting on a platter.

"What's new?" I asked Valerie.

"I've decided I'm going to have the baby. And I'm not getting married right away."

My mother made the sign of the cross, and her eyes wistfully drifted to the cupboard where she kept her Four Roses. The moment passed, and she took the pot roast into the dining room. "Let's eat," she said.

"How am I supposed to eat pot roast without teeth?" Grandma said. "If those teeth aren't returned by tomorrow morning, I'm calling the cops. I got a date for Christmas Eve. I invited my new boyfriend over for dinner."

We all froze. The studmuffin was coming to Christmas Eve dinner.

"Christ," my father said.

After dinner my mother gave me a bag filled with food. "I know you don't have time to cook," she said. It was part of the ritual. And someday, if I was lucky, I'd carry the tradition to a new generation. Except the bag to *my* daughter would probably be filled with take-out.

My father was outside, attaching the tree to my CRV. He was tying it to the roof rack, and every time he tightened the rope there was a shower of pine needles. "It might be a little dry," he said. "You should probably put it in water when you get home."

Halfway home I saw the lights behind me. Low-slung sporty car lights. I checked the rear-view mirror. Hard to see at night, but I was pretty sure it was a black Jag. I parked in the lot, and Diesel parked beside me. We both got out and looked at the tree. There was no moon-light, thank God.

"Can't hardly see it in the dark," Diesel said.

"It's better that way."

"How'd the stake-out go?"

"Like you said—quiet."

Diesel smiled when I told him the stake-out was quiet.

"I guess you know about the stake-out," I said with a sigh.

"Yup."

"How?"

"I know everything."

"Do not."

"Do so."

"Do not!"

There was a rush of wind, the air crackled, and Diesel grabbed me and threw me to the ground, covering me with his body. Light flashed and heat rippled over me for a moment. I heard Diesel swear and roll off. When I looked up I realized the tree was on fire. Sparks jumped against the black sky and the fire spread to the car.

Diesel pulled me to my feet, and we backed away from the flames. I was bummed about the car, but I wasn't all that unhappy to be rid of the tree.

"So, what do you think?" I asked Diesel. "Meteor?"

"Sorry, sunshine. That was meant for me."

I was standing facing my car, and behind me, I could hear windows being thrown open in my apartment building. It was Lorraine in her nightie and Mo in his cap. They'd just settled their brains for a long winter's nap in front of the television. When out in the lot there arose such a clatter, they sprang from their recliners to see what was the matter. Away to the window they flew like a flash, tore open the blinds and threw up the sash. And what to their wondering eyes should appear, but Stephanie Plum and yet another of her cars burning front to rear.

"Hey," Mo Kleinschmidt yelled. "Are you okay?"

I waved back at him.

"Nice touch with the tree," he yelled. "You never torched a tree before."

I glanced sideways at Diesel. "This isn't the first time one of my cars has been exploded, burned, or bombed."

"Gee, that's a big surprise," Diesel said.

Fire trucks screamed in the distance. Two patrol cars rolled into the lot, keeping a safe distance from the smoke and flames. Morelli pulled in behind the second patrol car. He got out of his truck and sauntered over. He looked at me, and then he looked at the toasted CRV. He gave his head a shake and a sigh escaped. Resignation. His girlfriend was a trial.

"I heard the call go out on the scanner, and I knew it had to be you," Morelli said. "Are you okay?"

"Yep. I'm fine. I figured this was the only way I'd get to see you."

"Funny," Morelli said. He checked Diesel out. "Do I have to worry about him?"

"No."

Morelli gave me a kiss on the top of the head. "I have to get back to the job."

Diesel and I watched him drive off.

"I like him," Diesel said. "I like the way he kisses you on the top of your head."

"Maybe you want to take your jacket off," I said to Diesel. "It's smoking."

NEXT MORNING, DIESEL was on the couch, watching television, when I got out of the shower. His presence was unexpected, and I had a brief moment of terror until my brain connected the dots between *big, uninvited man on couch* and *Diesel*.

"Jeez," I said. "Why don't you try using the doorbell? I wasn't expecting to find a man on my couch."

"Sounds like a personal problem," Diesel said. "What's the plan for the day?"

"I don't have a plan. I thought you'd have a plan."

"My plan is pretty much to follow you around. I figure there was a reason I was dropped here. So I'm waiting for it all to shake out."

Oh boy.

"There's some stuff for you in the kitchen," Diesel said. "The kerplunkers were picked over, but I got you a poinsettia and a Christmas tree. Seemed like I owed you a tree."

I went into the kitchen to investigate and found a nice big red poinsettia sitting on my counter. And a five-foot, fully decorated Christmas tree stood square in the middle of my kitchen floor. It was a live tree trimmed in gold and white, its base planted in a plastic tub swaddled in gold foil, the perfectly formed top of the tree capped with a star. It was gorgeous, but vaguely familiar. And then I remembered where I'd seen the tree. Quakerbridge Mall. The trees were strung along the entire ground floor of the shopping center.

"I'm afraid to ask where you got this tree," I said.

Diesel clicked the television off and ambled into the kitchen. "Yeah, some things are better left unknown."

"It's a nice tree. And it's all decorated."

"Hey, I deliver."

I was standing there admiring the tree, wondering if I could get jail time for being an accomplice to grand theft spruce, and Randy Briggs called.

"I just got in to work, and something strange is going on here. Your pal Sandy Claws showed up and sent everyone home. He shut down the whole production line."

"It's Christmas Eve day. He probably was just being nice."

"You don't get it. He shut down permanently."

"I thought you weren't going to rat for me."

"I just lost my job. You're the only thing between me and welfare."

"Are you still there?"

"I'm in the parking lot. It's just Claws and Lester inside."

"I'm on my way. Stick with Claws and Lester."

I hung up, grabbed my jacket and bag, and Diesel and I ran for the stairs. I paused for a moment when I pushed through the lobby doors and saw the charred spot on the pavement. No more CRV. Just some heat-scorched blacktop and a couple patches of ice where water had frozen.

Diesel snagged me by the sleeve and yanked me forward. "It was a car," he said. "It can be replaced."

I belted myself into the Jag. "It's not that simple. It takes time and money. And then there's the insurance." I didn't even want to *think* about the insurance. I was an insurance joke.

Diesel took off, flying low, heading for Route 1. "No problemo. What kind of car would you like? Another CRV? A truck? How about a Z3? I could see you in a Z3."

"No! I'll get my own car."

Diesel sailed through a red light and hit the on ramp to Route 1 south. "I bet you thought I was going to steal a car for you. In fact, I bet you thought I stole your Christmas tree."

"Well?"

"It's complicated," Diesel said, cutting into the far left lane, foot to the floor, looking far too calm for a guy going ninety.

I closed my eyes and tried to relax into my seat. If I was going to die in a fiery crash I didn't want to see it coming. "These superpowers you're supposed to have . . . they include driving, right?"

Diesel smiled and gave me a sideways glance. "Sure."

Damn. Not an answer that gave me confidence.

He took a corner with tires screaming, I opened my eyes and we were in the toy factory lot. Briggs was still there. And two other cars were parked close to the building entrance.

Diesel killed the engine and was out of the car. "Wait here."

"No way!" But my door was locked. *All* the car doors were locked. So I leaned on the horn.

Diesel wheeled around halfway to the factory entrance and sent me a warning glare, fists on hips. I kept my hand on the horn, and he did a disbelieving head shake. He walked back to the car, opened my door, and pulled me out. "You know, you're a real pain in the ass."

"Hey, without me, you'd be nowhere on this case."

He sighed and draped an arm across my shoulders. "Honey, I'm nowhere *with* you."

Another car door opened and closed, and Briggs joined us. "I'll come along in case you need muscle," Briggs said.

"If I get any more help I'll need a permit for a parade," Diesel said.

The reception area and front office cubbies were deserted. We found Sandy Claws and Lester, alone, in the back room where the toys were made. Lester and Claws were sitting together at one of the workstations. They looked over at us when we entered the room, but they didn't get up. There was a small block of wood in front of Claws, some shavings, and a couple woodworking tools. The corners had been shaved off the block of wood.

We walked over to the two men, and Diesel looked down at the wood. "What are you making?" he asked.

Claws smiled and ran his hand over the wood. "A special toy."

Diesel nodded as if he knew what that meant.

"Have you come to take me back?" Claws asked.

Diesel shook his head. "No. You're free to do whatever you want. I'm after Ring. Unfortunately, Ring is after *you*."

"Ring," Claws said with a sigh. "Who would have thought he had power left?"

"Looks to me like his aim is off," Diesel said.

"Cataracts. The old fool can't see."

Diesel scanned the room. Toys were scattered around, in various stages of completion. "You shut down the factory."

"He's out there," Claws said. "I can feel the electricity in the air. I couldn't take a chance on endangering the workers, so I sent them away."

"Good riddance," Lester said. "Nasty little slackards. They were more trouble than they were worth."

"The elves?" I asked.

Claws made a derisive sound. "We trucked them in from Newark. I rented this space sight unseen and then found out it used to be a day-care facility. Everything is sized for kids. I thought it would be cheaper to hire little people than to change out all the toilets and sinks. Problem was, we got a bunch of crazies. Half of them actually claimed to be elves. And you know how unmanageable elves can be."

We all nodded. "Yeah," we said in half-assed unison, "elves are flighty. You can't count on an elf."

"What will you do now?" Diesel asked.

Claws shrugged. "I'll make the occasional special toy. It's what I most enjoy, anyway."

"I'd like to put you and Elaine in a safer place until I get Ring under control," Diesel said.

"As long as Ring is at large, no place is safe," Claws said.

I cleared my throat and cracked my knuckles. "I sort of hate to bring this up right now, but I'm supposed to apprehend you." I reached into my bag and dragged out a pair of cuffs.

"Jeez," Briggs said.

"It's my job, remember?"

"Yeah, but it's Christmas Eve day. Cut the guy some slack."

"You don't get paid until I get paid," I told Briggs.

"Good point," Briggs said. "Cuff him."

I looked over at Diesel.

"It's your job," Diesel said.

I looked at the cuffs dangling from my hand. This was my last shot at Christmas present money. And bringing Claws in was the right thing to do. He'd broken the law and failed to appear for his court hearing. Problem was, it was Christmas Eve, and there was no guarantee I'd be able to get Claws bonded out again and released before everything shut down for the holiday. I thought about his house, bursting with baked goods and Christmas spirit, decorated with twinkle lights, blinking out best wishes to the world.

"I can't do it," I said. "It's Christmas Eve. Elaine would be alone with all those cookies."

Claws and Lester let out a whoosh of relief. Briggs looked conflicted. And Diesel grinned at me.

"Now what?" I asked.

"Now we hunt down Ring," Diesel said.

I didn't have to look at my watch to know it was midmorning. Time was oozing away from me. I had half a day to make Christmas happen. And some or all of that time was going to be spent hunting Ring. I could feel the panic sitting thick in my throat. I didn't even have the gloves I'd gotten for my dad. They'd gone up in smoke with the CRV.

"You could bail," Diesel said to me, reading my thoughts. "We'd understand."

Before I could make a decision there was a clap of thunder, the building shook, and a crack angled across the ceiling. We started for the door, but we were stopped midway by another *boom*. Plaster rained down from above, and we dove under a large butcher-block workstation. A couple large chunks of ceiling broke loose and crashed to the floor. More ceiling followed. The light blinked out, and demolition dust swirled around us. The workstation table had saved our lives, but we were buried under debris from the roof.

We did a head count and concluded we were all okay.

"I could dig my way through this mess," Diesel said, "but I'm afraid it's unstable. It needs to be cleared from the top."

We all tried our cell phones, but we had no reception.

"I don't get it," Briggs said. "What was that? It felt like an earthquake, but we don't get earthquakes in Jersey."

"I guess it was a . . . phenomenon," I said.

We sat there for a half hour, waiting for the sound of fire trucks and emergency equipment.

"No one knows we're trapped here," Claws finally said. "We're separated from the other businesses by parking lots and roadways. And most of the businesses here are storage facilities with minimum traffic."

"And it's possible the ceiling collapsed but the walls are still standing," Lester said. "If someone doesn't look closely they might not see the damage."

I inched closer to Diesel. He felt big and safe and solid.

He playfully tugged at a strand of my hair. "You aren't scared, are you?" he asked me, his lips skimming across my ear.

"Not me. Nope. I'm cool."

Liar, liar, pants on fire. I was scared beyond all reason. I was trapped under a ton of rubble with four men and no bathroom. My heart was beating with a sickening thud in my chest, and I was cold to the bone with fear and claustrophobia. If I got out alive I'd probably have a few uncomfortable moments remembering the way Diesel's mouth had felt on my ear. Right now, I was trying to keep my teeth from chattering in panic.

"Someone needs to go for help," Claws said.

"I guess that would be me," Diesel said. "Don't anyone freak."

There was a sound like a soap bubble bursting. *Plink.* And I no longer felt Diesel beside me.

"Holy crap," Briggs said, "what was that?"

"Uh, I don't know," I said.

"We're all still here, right?" Briggs asked.

"I'm here," I said.

"I didn't hear anything," Lester said.

"Yeah, me either," Briggs said. "I didn't hear anything."

We sat and waited in the eerie quiet.

"Hello," Briggs called after a while, but no one answered, and we all fell silent again.

There was no way to assess time in the pitch-black cave. Minutes dragged by, and then suddenly there was a faraway sound. Scraping and clunking. And muffled voices carried in to us. We heard sirens, but they were faint, the sound deadened by the debris.

Two hours later, after I'd made a lot of deals with God, a large piece of ceiling was hauled off our table, and we saw daylight and faces peering in at us. Another piece was removed, and Diesel dropped through the opening.

"I'm thinking that I just imagined you were trapped under the ceiling with us," Briggs said. "You were actually on the outside all the time, right?"

"Right," Diesel said, reaching for me.

He gave me a boost, a couple firemen pulled me through the hole, and a cheer went up. Briggs came next, then Lester, then Claws, and finally Diesel emerged.

Pretty much the entire roof had collapsed, but as Lester had suggested, the walls were still standing. The lot was filled with emergency vehicles and the curious. I stood in the lot and shook my head and plaster dust flew off. My clothes were caked with it, and I could still taste the dust in the back of my throat.

I looked over at Claws and realized for the first time that he'd taken his toy-in-progress with him when the building started to collapse. He had it cradled in his arm, held close to his chest. It was a small, half-carved block of wood, covered in dust, just like the rest of us. Too early for me to tell what sort of toy he was making. I watched him slip past the first line of rescue workers and quietly get into his car and drive off. Smart move, since he was wanted for failing to appear.

I looked around the lot. And then I looked into the sky.

"He isn't here," Diesel said to me. "He doesn't hang around after he strikes."

"What does he look like?" In my mind I was envisioning the Green Goblin.

"Just a normal, little old guy with cataracts."

"No utility belt? No lightning bolt embroidered on his shirt?"

"Sorry."

An EMT draped a blanket around my shoulders and tried to guide me to a truck. I looked at my watch and dug my heels in. "Can't get checked out right now," I said. "Gotta shop."

"You don't look that great," the guy said. "You're kind of pale."

"Of course I'm pale. There are only four

shopping hours left before I'm due at my parents' house for Christmas Eve dinner. You'd look pale too if you were in my shoes." I turned to Diesel. "I had time to do some serious thinking while I was trapped under the table, and things became very clear to me. My mother is more of a threat to me right now than Ring. Take me to Macy's!"

It was midafternoon and the roads were relatively empty. Businesses had shut down early. Kids were on vacation. Shoppers were retiring their credit cards. Jersey was at home, preparing the holiday beast for Christmas Day dinner, gearing up for an evening of toy assembly and package wrapping. In eight hours, when the stores are all closed, the entire population of the state will be in desperate search for batteries, wrapping paper, and tape.

In eight hours, children statewide will be listening for reindeer hooves on the roof. Except for Mary Alice, who no longer believed in Christmas.

Anticipation hung in the air over the mall, the highway, the Burg, and every house in every town that mashed together to form the megalopolis. Christmas was almost here. Like it, or not.

Diesel swung into the lot and got a space close to the mall entrance. No problem with parking now. Inside the mall, the silence was oppressive. Shell-shocked salesclerks stood motionless, waiting for the closing bell. A few customers staggered from rack to rack. Men, mostly. Looking lost.

"Cripes," Diesel said. "This is frightening. This is like being with the living dead."

"What about you?" I asked. "Is your Christmas shopping all done?"

"I don't do a lot of Christmas shopping."

"Wife, girlfriend, mother?"

"I'm currently without."

"I'm sorry."

He tweaked my nose and smiled. "It's okay. I've got *you*."

"Did you get me a present?"

Our eyes locked, and his expression warmed a couple notches. He raised his eyebrows ever so slightly in question, and I felt my temperature rise.

"Do you *want* a present?" he asked. Both of us understanding what he was offering.

"No. Nope." I sucked in some air and busied myself, brushing some dust off my jacket. "Thanks, anyway."

"Let me know if you change your mind," he said, his voice back to playful.

Ordinarily, two people walking through Quakerbridge covered in construction dust would attract some attention. At four o'clock on Christmas Eve, no one would have noticed if we'd been naked. I didn't waste time on details such as the right size or color. I went with Lula's method. Fill your bag with stuff close to the register. I finished up at five-thirty, and I wrapped the presents on the way to my parents' house.

Diesel jerked to a stop at the curb, and we tumbled out of the car with our arms full of boxes and bags.

Grandma was at the door. "She's here," she called to the rest of the family. "And she's got that hunky sissy boy with her again."

"Sissy boy?" Diesel asked.

"It's complicated," I said.

"Omigod," my mother said when she saw us. "What happened? You're filthy."

"It's nothing," I said. "A building fell down on us, and we didn't have time to change."

"A couple years ago I would have thought that was unusual," my mother said.

"You've gotta help me," Grandma said. "My studmuffin is coming to dinner, and I still haven't got my teeth."

"We've looked everywhere," my mother said. "We even looked through the garbage."

"Someone stole them," Grandma said. "I bet a good set of teeth would bring a pretty penny on the black market."

There was a knock at the door, and Morelli let himself in.

"Just the person I want to see," Grandma said. "I want to report a crime. Someone stole my teeth."

Morelli looked over at me. The first look said, *help*. And the second look said *what the hell happened to you?*

"A ceiling sort of fell in on us," I told Morelli. "But we're fine."

A muscle worked in Morelli's jaw. He was trying to stay calm.

"Where were your teeth when you saw them last?" I asked Grandma.

"In a glass, getting cleaned."

"Did you lose just the teeth? Or is the glass gone, too?"

"The lousy rotten robber took everything, glass and all."

Mary Alice and Angie were in front of the television.

"Hey," I said to them. "Either of you see Grandma's teeth? They were in a glass in the kitchen and now they're missing."

"I thought Grammy was throwing them away, so I took them for Charlotte," Mary Alice said.

Charlotte is a big lavender dinosaur that lives in Grandma's bedroom. Grandma won

Charlotte at the Point Pleasant boardwalk two years ago. Grandma put four quarters down on number thirty-one, red. The guy spun the game wheel. And Grandma won Charlotte. Charlotte had originally been intended for Mary Alice, but Grandma got attached to Charlotte and kept her. Some of the stuffing has shifted in Charlotte's big dino body, so she has lumpy spots now . . . kind of like Grandma.

Mary Alice ran upstairs and retrieved Charlotte. And sure enough, the teeth were nicely set into Charlotte's gaping mouth.

"Charlotte's teeth had lost their stuffing," Mary Alice said. "And Charlotte was having trouble eating, so I gave her Grandma's teeth."

"Isn't that something," Grandma said. "I never noticed."

We all looked more closely at the teeth. They were decorated with flowers and tiny rainbows and colorful stars.

"I made the teeth more pretty with my markers," Mary Alice said. "I used the water-proof ones so they wouldn't wash off."

"That's nice, honey," Grandma said, "but I need my choppers on account of I've got a hot date tonight. I'll get Charlotte some teeth of her own."

Grandma took the teeth from Charlotte and

put them into her mouth. Grandma smiled, and we all tried to stifle ourselves. Except for my father.

"Holy crap," my father said, staring transfixed at Grandma's decorated teeth.

The phone rang and Grandma ran to answer it. "It was my studmuffin," Grandma said when she hung up. "He said he had a hard day, and he needs to take a nap and recharge his battery. So we're going to meet up at Stiva's after dinner. There's going to be a special Christmas Eve viewing for Betty Schlimmer."

We always had baked ham for Christmas. The ham was hot on Christmas Eve, and for Christmas Day my mom would set out a big buffet with cold sliced ham and macaroni and about a billion other dishes.

Kloughn arrived just as we were sitting down to the table. "Am I late?" he asked. "I hope I'm not late. I tried not to be late, but there was an accident on Hamilton Avenue. A really good one. Legitimate neck injuries and everything. I think they might hire me." He kissed Valerie on the cheek and blushed bright red. "Are you okay?" he asked. "Did you throw up a lot today? Are you feeling any better? Boy, I sure wish you'd feel better."

Grandma passed Kloughn the mashed potatoes. "I hear those neck injuries can be worth a lot of money," Grandma said.

Kloughn looked at Grandma's teeth, and the potato spoon dropped out of his hand and clattered onto his plate. "Ulk," Kloughn said.

"You're probably wondering about my teeth," Grandma said to Kloughn. "Mary Alice decorated them for me."

"I've never seen decorated teeth before. I've seen decorated nails. And people get tattoos all over the place, right? So I guess decorated teeth could be the next big thing," Kloughn said. "Maybe I should get my teeth decorated. I wonder if I could get fish painted on them. What do you think about fish?"

"Rainbow trout would be good," Grandma said. "That way you could have lots of colors."

Mary Alice was fidgeting in her chair. She was softly talking to herself, twisting her hair around and around her index finger, wriggling on her seat.

"What's the matter?" Grandma asked. "Do you need to gallop?"

Mary Alice looked to my mother.

"Go for it," my mother said. "It's been too quiet around here. I think we need a horse to liven things up."

"I know there isn't any Santa Claus," Mary Alice said, "but if there *was*, do you think he'd give presents to a horse?"

We all jumped right in.

"Absolutely."

"Of course."

"You bet."

"Darn tootin', he'd give presents to a horse."

Mary Alice stopped fidgeting and looked thoughtful. "I was just wondering," she said.

Angie watched Mary Alice. "There *might* be a Santa," Angie said, very seriously.

Mary Alice stared at her plate. There were weighty decisions to be made here.

Mary Alice wasn't the only one caught between a rock and a hard place. I had Diesel on one side of me and Morelli on the other, and I could feel the pull of their personalities. They weren't competing. Diesel was in an entirely different place from Morelli. It was more that their energy fields were intersecting over my air space.

Grandma jumped up halfway through dessert. "Look at the time," she said. "I gotta go. Bitsy Greenfield's picking me up, and she'll go without me if I'm not ready. We gotta get there early for this one. It's a special ceremony. It'll be standing room only."

"Maybe you shouldn't do too much talking," I said to Grandma. "People might not understand about the artwork on your teeth."

"No problem," she said. "Nobody in that crowd can see good enough to know anything's different. What with everyone having macular degeneration and cataracts, I don't have to even wear makeup. Being old has a lot of advantages. Everybody looks good when you got cataracts."

"Okay, so tell me again why this guy is your new best friend," Morelli said. We were outside on the small back porch, flapping our arms to keep warm. It was the only place to have a private conversation.

"He's looking for a guy named Ring. And he thinks Ring is somehow connected to me. But we don't know how. So he's staying close to me until we figure it out."

"How close?"

"Not that close."

Inside the house my parents and sister were dragging presents out from hiding places and arranging them under the tree. Angie and Mary Alice were sound asleep. Grandma was off somewhere, presumably with her studmuffin. And Diesel had been sent in search of batteries.

"I have a present for you," Morelli said, curling his fingers into my coat collar, pulling me to him.

"Is it a big present?"

"No. It's a small present."

So that eliminated the first item on my Christmas wish list.

Morelli gave me a little box, wrapped in red foil. I opened the box and found a ring. It was composed of slim intertwined gold and platinum bands. Set into the bands were three small deep blue sapphires. "It's a friendship ring," Morelli said. "We tried the engagement thing, and that didn't work."

"Not yet, anyway," I told him.

"Yeah, not yet," he said, sliding the ring onto my finger.

Sound carried crystal clear on the cold air. I heard a car pull up to the curb. A door opened and closed. And then a second.

"Aren't you the one," Grandma said.

The deeper male voice didn't carry back to us as clearly.

"It's Grandma and the studmuffin!" I whispered to Morelli.

"Listen," Morelli said, "I'd really like to stay but I've got this assignment . . ."

I opened the kitchen door. "Forget it. You're staying. I'm not facing the studmuffin alone."

"Look who I've got," Grandma announced to everyone. "This here's my friend John."

He was about five-foot-nine, with white hair, a ruddy complexion, and a slim build. He wore thick-lensed glasses and was dressed for the occasion in neatly pressed gray slacks, casual rubber-soled shoes, and a red blazer. Truth is, Grandma had dragged home a lot worse. If John had artificial parts, he was keeping them to himself. Fine by me.

Grandma didn't look nearly so well groomed. Her lipstick was smeared, and her hair was standing on end.

"Yikes," Morelli whispered to me.

I extended my hand to the studmuffin. "I'm Stephanie," I said.

He shook my hand and my scalp tingled and a tiny spark passed between us. "I'm John Ring," he said.

Oh boy. So this is the connection. This is the reason Diesel was dropped into my kitchen.

"He's just full of static electricity tonight," Grandma said. "We're gonna have to rub him down with one of them fabric softener sheets."

"I'm sorry I couldn't make dinner," Ring said. "I had a stressful day." He stepped closer, adjusted his glasses, and squinted at me. "Do I know you? You seem familiar, somehow."

"She's a bounty hunter," Grandma said. "She tracks down bad guys."

Zzzzzt. A series of sparks crackled off Ring's head.

"Isn't that something the way he can do

that?" Grandma said. "He's been doing that all night."

My mother slyly made the sign of the cross and took a step backward. Morelli moved closer to me, pressing himself against my back, his hand at the nape of my neck.

"Look at the hair on my arm," Kloughn said. "It's all standing up. Why do you suppose it's doing that? Boy, I'm kind of creeped out. Do you suppose it means something? What do you suppose it means?"

"The air's real dry," I said. "Sometimes hair doesn't lie down when the air's real dry."

Here I was, face to face with Ring, Diesel was off hunting batteries, and I hadn't a clue what to do. My heart was skipping beats, and I was humming from head to toe. I could feel vibrations coming through the soles of my shoes.

"I feel like a Slurpee," I said to Grandma and Ring. "How about we all go to 7-Eleven and get a Slurpee?"

"Now?" Grandma said. "We just got here."

"Yep. *Now*. I really need a Slurpee."

What I needed was to get Ring out of my parents' house. I didn't want him near Angie and Mary Alice. I didn't want him near my mom and dad.

"Maybe you could stay here and help wrap

presents," I said to Grandma. "And Mr. Ring could give me a ride to 7-Eleven. It would give us a chance to get acquainted."

Zzzzt. Zzzzzt. Mr. Ring didn't seem to like that idea.

"Just a suggestion," I said.

Morelli's hand was steady at my neck, and Ring took a couple deep breaths.

"Are you okay?" Grandma asked Ring. "You don't look too good."

"I'm . . . excited," he said. "M-m-meeting your family." *Zzzt.*

It looked to me like Ring was having a control problem. He was leaking electricity. And he seemed as uncomfortable with his position as I was.

"Well," he said, forcing a smile, "this is a typical fun family Christmas, isn't it?" *Zzzzt.* He wiped a bead of sweat from his forehead. *Zzzt. Zzzt.* "And this is your lovely Christmas tree."

"I paid fifteen bucks for it," my father said. *Zzzt.*

The tree had about twelve needles left on it and was tinder dry. My father diligently watered it every day, but this tree died in July.

Ring reached out, tentatively touched the tree, and it burst into flames.

"Holy shit," Kloughn yelped. "Fire. *Fire!* Get

the kids out of the house. Get the dog. Get the ham."

The fire spread to the cotton batting wrapped around the base of the tree and then to the presents. A streak of fire raced up a nearby curtain.

"Call 911," my mother said. "Call the fire company. Frank, get the fire extinguisher from the kitchen!"

My dad turned to the kitchen, but Morelli already had the extinguisher in hand. Moments later, we all stood dazed, mouths agape, staring at the mess. The tree was gone. The presents were gone. The curtain was in tatters.

John Ring was gone.

And Diesel hadn't returned.

There was a loud series of explosions outside and through the window we saw the sky light up, bright as day. And then all was dark and quiet.

"Cripes," my dad said.

Grandma looked around. "Where's John? Where's my studmuffin?"

"You mean Sparky," Kloughn said. "Get it? Sparky?"

"Looks like he left," I said.

"Hunh, just like a man," Grandma said. "Burn down your Christmas tree and then up and leave."

Morelli set the fire extinguisher aside and crooked his arm around my neck. "Is there anything you want to tell me?"

"I don't think so."

"I didn't see any of this," Morelli said. "I didn't see the sparks coming off his head. And I didn't see him set the tree on fire."

"Me either," I told him. "I didn't see any of that stuff, either."

We all stood there for some more long moments with nothing to say. There were no words. Just shock. And maybe some denial.

A small, sleepy voice broke the silence.

"What happened?" Mary Alice asked.

She was on the stairs in her jammies. Angie was behind her.

"We had a fire," my mom said.

Mary Alice and Angie approached the tree. Mary Alice studied the charred boxes. She looked up at my mom. "Were these presents from the family?"

"Yes."

Mary Alice was sober. Thinking. She looked at Angie. And she looked at Grandma.

"That's good," she finally said, "because I'd hate to have Santa's presents get burned." Mary Alice climbed onto the couch and sat with her hands folded in her lap. "I'm going to wait for Santa," she said.

"I thought you didn't believe in Santa," Grandma said.

"Diesel said it's important to believe in things that make you happy. He was in my room just now, and he said he was going away, but Santa Claus would come to visit tonight."

"Did he have a horse with him?" Grandma asked. "Or a reindeer?"

Mary Alice shook her head. "It was just Diesel."

Angie climbed next to Mary Alice. "I'll wait, too."

"We should clean this mess up," Grandma said.

"Tomorrow," my mother told her, taking a dining room chair into the living room, sitting across from Mary Alice and Angie. "I'm going to wait for Santa."

So we all sat and waited for Santa. We put the television on but we weren't really watching. We were listening for footsteps on the roof. Hoping to catch a glimpse of reindeer flying past the window. Waiting for something magical to happen.

The clock struck twelve and I heard cars drive up and doors open and close. And I heard voices, babbling in hushed excitement. There was a knock on the front door and we all jumped to our feet. I answered the door and wasn't too surprised to see Sandy Claws. He was dressed in a snappy red suit with a red Christmas tie. He held a box, all wrapped up in shiny paper and tied with a golden bow. Behind him squirmed a legion of elves. (Who was I to say if they were fake or real?) All bearing presents. Randy Briggs was among them.

"Diesel said you needed some help with Christmas," Claws said to me.

"Is he okay?"

"He's fine. Diesel is always fine. He's returning Ring to the Home."

"How can he do that? How can he get around the electricity stuff?"

"Diesel has ways."

"I bet you get harassed, right?" Kloughn said to a couple of the elves. "I bet you could use a good lawyer. Let me give you my card."

My mother rushed to the kitchen and returned with platters of cookies and fruitcake. My father cracked out some beer. Grandma eyed Claws.

"He's a cutie," she said to me. "Do you know if he's taken?"

The party lasted until all the presents were opened, the last cookie was eaten, the last beer swilled. The elves said their good-byes and packed off in their cars. Sandy Claws and

Briggs remained with one last box. It was the box with the golden bow, and Claws gave the box to Mary Alice.

"I made this myself," he said. "Just for you. Keep it always. It's a special present for a very special person."

Mary Alice opened the box and looked inside. "It's beautiful," she said.

It was a horse. Carved from curly cherry wood.

Mary Alice held it in her hand. "It's warm," she said.

I felt the horse. It was cool to my touch. I raised eyebrows in question to Sandor.

"A special present for a special person," he said to me.

"A special person with special abilities?"

He smiled. "There are signs."

I smiled back at him.

"See you in court," he said.

I AWOKE AT dawn and gently slid away from Morelli. I padded through my dark apartment to the kitchen. The mall tree was lit with tiny twinkle lights, and Diesel was leaning against the counter.

"Is this good-bye?" I asked him.

"Until next time." He took my hand and

kissed my palm. "It was a good Christmas," he said. "See you around, sunshine."

"See you around," I said, but he was already gone.

And he was dead-on right, I thought. It was a *very* good Christmas.

**ST. MARTIN'S PRESS INVITES
YOU TO DISCOVER THE
"ONE" THAT STARTED IT ALL**

ONE FOR THE MONEY

THERE ARE SOME men who enter a woman's life and screw it up forever. Joseph Morelli did this to me—not forever, but periodically.

Morelli and I were both born and raised in a blue-collar chunk of Trenton called the Burg. Houses were attached and narrow. Yards were small. Cars were American. The people were mostly of Italian descent, with enough Hungarians and Germans thrown in to offset inbreeding. It was a good place to buy calzone or play the numbers. And, if you had to live in Trenton anyway, it was an okay place to raise a family.

When I was a kid I didn't ordinarily play with Joseph Morelli. He lived two blocks over and was two years older. "Stay away from those Morelli boys," my mother had warned me. "They're wild. I hear stories about the things they do to girls when they get them alone."

"What kind of things?" I'd eagerly asked.

"You don't want to know," my mother had answered. "Terrible things. Things that aren't nice."

From that moment on, I viewed Joseph Morelli with a combination of terror and prurient curiosity that bordered on awe. Two weeks later, at the age of six, with quaking knees and a squishy stomach, I followed Morelli into his father's garage on the promise of learning a new game.

The Morelli garage hunkered detached and snubbed at the edge of their lot. It was a sorry affair, lit by a single shaft of light filtering through a grime-coated window. Its air was stagnant, smelling of corner must, discarded tires, and jugs of used motor oil. Never destined to house the Morelli cars, the garage served other purposes. Old Man Morelli used the garage to take his belt to his sons, his sons used the garage to take their hands to themselves, and Joseph Morelli took me, Stephanie Plum, to the garage to play train.

"What's the name of this game?" I'd asked Joseph Morelli.

"Choo-choo," he'd said, down on his hands and knees, crawling between my legs, his head trapped under my short pink skirt. "You're the tunnel, and I'm the train."

I suppose this tells something about my personality. That I'm not especially good at taking advice. Or that I was born with an overload of curiosity. Or maybe it's about rebellion or boredom or fate. At any rate, it was a one-shot deal and darn disappointing, since I'd only gotten to be the tunnel, and I'd really wanted to be the train.

Ten years later, Joe Morelli was still living two blocks over. He'd grown up big and bad, with eyes like black fire one minute and melt-in-your-mouth chocolate the next. He had an eagle tattooed on his chest, a tight-assed, narrow-hipped swagger, and a reputation for having fast hands and clever fingers.

My best friend, Mary Lou Molnar, said she heard Morelli had a tongue like a lizard.

"Holy cow," I'd answered, "what's that supposed to mean?"

"Just don't let him get you alone or you'll find out. Once he gets you alone . . . that's it. You're done for."

I hadn't seen much of Morelli since the train episode. I supposed he'd enlarged his repertoire of sexual exploitation. I opened my eyes wide and leaned closer to Mary Lou, hoping for the worst. "You aren't talking about rape, are you?"

"I'm talking about lust! If he wants you, you're doomed. The guy is irresistible."

Aside from being fingered at the age of six by you-know-who, I was untouched. I was saving myself for marriage, or at least for college. "I'm a virgin," I said, as if this was news. "I'm sure he doesn't mess with virgins."

"He specializes in virgins! The brush of his fingertips turns virgins into slobbering mush."

Two weeks later, Joe Morelli came into the bakery where I worked every day after school, Tasty Pastry, on Hamilton. He bought a chocolate-chip cannoli, told me he'd joined the navy, and charmed the pants off me four minutes after closing, on the floor of Tasty Pastry, behind the case filled with chocolate éclairs.

The next time I saw him, I was three years older. I was on my way to the mall, driving my father's Buick when I spotted Morelli standing in front of Giovichinni's Meat Market. I gunned the big V-8 engine, jumped the curb, and clipped Morelli from behind, bouncing him off the front right fender. I stopped the car and got out to assess the damage. "Anything broken?"

He was sprawled on the pavement, looking up my skirt. "My leg."

"Good," I said. Then I turned on my heel,

got into the Buick, and drove to the mall.

I attribute the incident to temporary insanity, and in my own defense, I'd like to say I haven't run over anyone since.

DURING WINTER MONTHS, wind ripped up Hamilton Avenue, whining past plate-glass windows, banking trash against curbs and storefronts. During summer months, the air sat still and gauzy, leaden with humidity, saturated with hydrocarbons. It shimmered over hot cement and melted road tar. Cicadas buzzed, Dumpsters reeked, and a dusty haze hung in perpetuity over softball fields statewide. I figured it was all part of the great adventure of living in New Jersey.

This afternoon I'd decided to ignore the August buildup of ozone catching me in the back of my throat and go, convertible top down, in my Mazda Miata. The air conditioner was blasting flat out, I was singing along with Paul Simon, my shoulder-length brown hair was whipping around my face in a frenzy of frizz and snarls, my ever vigilant blue eyes were coolly hidden behind my Oakleys, and my foot rested heavy on the gas pedal.

It was Sunday, and I had a date with a pot roast at my parents' house. I stopped for a light and checked my rearview mirror, swearing when I saw Lenny Gruber two car lengths back in a tan sedan. I thunked my forehead on the steering wheel. "Damn." I'd gone to high school with Gruber. He was a maggot then, and he was a maggot now. Unfortunately, he was a maggot with a just cause. I was behind on my Miata payments, and Gruber worked for the repo company.

Six months ago, when I'd bought the car, I'd been looking good, with a nice apartment and season tickets to the Rangers. And then *bam*! I got laid off. No money. No more A-1 credit rating.

I rechecked the mirror, set my teeth, and yanked up the emergency brake. Lenny was like smoke. When you tried to grab him, he evaporated, so I wasn't about to waste this one last opportunity to bargain. I hauled myself out of my car, apologized to the man caught between us, and stalked back to Gruber.

"Stephanie Plum," Gruber said, full of joy and faux surprise. "What a treat."

I leaned two hands on the roof and looked through the open window at him. "Lenny, I'm going to my parents' house for dinner. You wouldn't snatch my car while I was at my parents' house, would you? I mean, that would be really low, Lenny."

"I'm a pretty low guy, Steph. That's why I've got this neat job. I'm capable of most anything."

The light changed, and the driver behind Gruber leaned on his horn.

"Maybe we can make a deal," I said to Gruber.

"Does this deal involve you getting naked?"

I had a vision of grabbing his nose and twisting it Three Stooges style until he squealed like a pig. Problem was, it'd involve touching him. Better to go with a more restrained approach. "Let me keep the car tonight, and I'll drive it to the lot first thing tomorrow morning."

"No way," Gruber said. "You're damn sneaky. I've been chasing after this car for five days."

"So, one more won't matter."

"I'd expect you to be grateful, you know what I mean?"

I almost gagged. "Forget it. Take the car. In fact, you could take it right now. I'll walk to my parents'."

Gruber's eyes were locked halfway down my chest. I'm a 36B. Respectable but far from overwhelming on my 5' 7" frame. I was wearing black spandex shorts and an oversized hockey jersey. Not what you would call a seductive outfit, but Lenny was ogling anyway.

His smile widened enough to show he was missing a molar. "I guess I could wait for tomorrow. After all, we *did* go to high school together."

"Uh huh." It was the best I could do.

Five minutes later I turned off Hamilton onto Roosevelt. Two blocks to my parents' house, and I could feel familial obligation sucking at me, pulling me into the heart of the Burg. This was a community of extended families. There was safety here, along with love, and stability, and the comfort of ritual. The clock on the dash told me I was seven minutes late, and the urge to scream told me I was home.

I parked at the curb and looked at the narrow two-story duplex with its jalousied front porch and aluminum awnings. The Plum half was yellow, just as it had been for forty years, with a brown shingle roof. Snowball bushes flanked either side of the cement stoop, and red geraniums had been evenly spaced the length of the porch. It was basically a flat. Living room in front, dining room in the middle, kitchen at the rear. Three bedrooms and bath upstairs. It was a small, tidy house crammed with kitchen smells and too much furniture, comfortable with its lot in life.

Next door, Mrs. Markowitz, who was living on Social Security and could only afford close-out paint colors, had painted her side lime green.

My mother was at the open screen door. "Stephanie," she called. "What are you doing sitting out there in your car? You're late for dinner. You know how your father hates to eat late. The potatoes are getting cold. The pot roast will be dry."

Food is important in the Burg. The moon revolves around the earth, the earth revolves around the sun, and the Burg revolves around pot roast. For as long as I can remember, my parents' lives have been controlled by five-pound pieces of rolled rump, done to perfection at six o'clock.

Grandma Mazur stood two feet back from my mother. "I gotta get me a pair of those," she said, eyeballing my shorts. "I've still got pretty good legs, you know." She raised her skirt and looked down at her knees. "What do you think? You think I'd look good in them biker things?"

Grandma Mazur had knees like doorknobs. She'd been a beauty in her time, but the years had turned her slack-skinned and spindle-boned. Still, if she wanted to wear biker shorts, I thought she should go for it. The way I saw it, that was one of the many advantages to living in New Jersey—even old ladies were allowed to look outlandish.

My father gave a grunt of disgust from the kitchen, where he was carving up the meat. "Biker's shorts," he muttered, slapping his palm against his forehead. "Unh!"

Two years ago, when Grandpa Mazur's fat-clogged arteries sent him to the big pork roast in the sky, Grandma Mazur had moved in with my parents and had never moved out. My father accepted this with a combination of Old-World stoicism and tactless mutterings.

I remember him telling me about a dog he'd had as a kid. The story goes that this dog was the ugliest, oldest, most pea-brained dog ever. The dog was incontinent, dribbling urine wherever it went. Its teeth were rotted in its mouth, its hips were fused solid with arthritis, and huge fatty tumors lumped under its hide. One day my Grandpa Plum took the dog out behind the garage and shot it. I suspected there were times when my father fantasized a similar ending for my Grandma Mazur.

"You should wear a dress," my mother said to me, bringing green beans and creamed pearl onions to the table. "Thirty years old and you're still dressing in those teeny-bopper outfits. How will you ever catch a nice man like that?"

"I don't want a man. I had one, and I didn't like it."

"That's because your husband was a horse's behind," Grandma Mazur said.

I agreed. My ex-husband had been a horse's behind. Especially when I'd caught him flagrante delicto on the dining room table with Joyce Barnhardt.

"I hear Loretta Buzick's boy is separated from his wife," my mother said. "You remember him? Ronald Buzick?"

I knew where she was heading, and I didn't want to go there. "I'm not going out with Ronald Buzick," I told her. "Don't even think about it."

"So what's wrong with Ronald Buzick?"

Ronald Buzick was a butcher. He was balding, and he was fat, and I suppose I was being a snob about the whole thing, but I found it hard to think in romantic terms about a man who spent his days stuffing giblets up chicken butts.

My mother plunged on. "All right, then how about Bernie Kuntz? I saw Bernie Kuntz in the dry cleaners, and he made a point about asking for you. I think he's interested. I could invite him over for coffee and cake."

With the way my luck was running, probably my mother had already invited Bernie, and at this very moment he was circling the block, popping Tic Tacs. "I don't want to talk about

Bernie," I said. "There's something I need to tell you. I have some bad news. . . ."

I'd been dreading this and had put it off for as long as possible.

My mother clapped a hand to her mouth. "You found a lump in your breast!"

No one in our family had ever found a lump in their breast, but my mother was ever watchful. "My breast is fine. The problem is with my job."

"What about your job?"

"I don't have one. I got laid off."

"Laid off!" she said on a sharp inhale. "How could that happen? It was such a good job. You loved that job."

I'd been a discount lingerie buyer for E.E. Martin, and I'd worked in Newark, which is not exactly the garden spot of the Garden State. In truth, it had been my mother who had loved the job, imagining it to be glamorous when in reality I'd mostly haggled over the cost of full-fashion nylon underpants. E.E. Martin wasn't exactly Victoria's Secret.

"I wouldn't worry," my mother said. "There's always work for lingerie buyers."

"There's *no* work for lingerie buyers." Especially ones who worked for E.E. Martin. Having held a salaried position with E.E. Martin made me as appealing as a leper. E.E. Martin had skimped on the palm greasing this winter, and as a result its mob affiliations were made public. The C.E.O. was indicted for illegal business practices, E.E. Martin sold out to Baldicott, Inc., and, through no fault of my own, I was caught in the house-cleaning sweep. "I've been out of work for six months."

"Six months! And I didn't know! Your own mother didn't know you were out on the streets?"

"I'm not out on the streets. I've been doing temporary jobs. Filing and stuff." And steadily sliding downhill. I was registered with every search firm in the greater Trenton area, and I religiously read the want ads. I wasn't being all that choosy, drawing the line at telephone soliciting and kennel attendant, but my future didn't look great. I was overqualified for entry level, and I lacked experience in management.

My father forked another slab of pot roast onto his plate. He'd worked for the post office for thirty years and had opted for early retirement. Now he drove a cab part-time.

"I saw your cousin Vinnie yesterday," he said. "He's looking for someone to do filing. You should give him a call."

Just the career move I'd been hoping for—filing for Vinnie. Of all my relatives, Vinnie was my least favorite. Vinnie was a worm, a sexual lunatic, a dog turd. "What does he pay?" I asked.

My father shrugged. "Gotta be minimum wage."

Wonderful. The perfect position for someone already in the depths of despair. Rotten boss, rotten job, rotten pay. The possibilities for feeling sorry for myself would be endless.

"And the best part is that it's close," my mother said. "You can come home every day for lunch."

I nodded numbly, thinking I'd sooner stick a needle in my eye.

SUNLIGHT SLANTED THROUGH the crack in my bedroom curtains, the air-conditioning unit in the living room window droned ominously, predicting another scorcher of a morning, and the digital display on my clock radio flashed electric blue numbers, telling me it was nine o'clock. The day had started without me.

I rolled out of bed on a sigh and shuffled into the bathroom. When I was done in the bathroom, I shuffled into the kitchen and stood in front of the refrigerator, hoping the refrigerator fairies had visited during the night. I opened the door and stared at the empty shelves, noting that food hadn't magically cloned itself from the smudges in the butter keeper and the shriveled flotsam at the bottom of the crisper. Half a jar of mayo, a bottle of beer, whole-wheat bread covered with blue mold, a head of iceberg lettuce, shrink-wrapped in brown slime and plastic, and a box of hamster nuggets stood between me and starvation. I wondered if nine in the morning was too early to drink beer. Of course in Moscow it would be four in the afternoon. Good enough.

I drank half the beer and grimly approached the living room window. I pulled the curtains and stared down at the parking lot. My Miata was gone. Lenny had hit early. No surprise, but still, it lodged painfully in the middle of my throat. I was now an official deadbeat.

And if that wasn't depressing enough, I'd weakened halfway through dessert and promised my mother I'd go see Vinnie.

I dragged myself into the shower and stumbled out a half hour later after an exhausting crying jag. I stuffed myself into pantyhose and a suit and was ready to do my daughterly duty.

My hamster, Rex, was still asleep in his soup can in his cage on the kitchen counter. I dropped a few hamster nuggets into his bowl and made some smoochy sounds. Rex opened his black eyes and blinked. He twitched his whiskers, gave a good sniff, and rejected the nuggets. I couldn't blame him. I'd tried them for breakfast yesterday and hadn't been impressed.

I locked up the apartment and walked three blocks down St. James to Blue Ribbon Used Cars. At the front of the lot was a $500 Nova begging to be bought. Total body rust and countless accidents had left the Nova barely recognizable as a car, much less a Chevy, but Blue Ribbon was willing to trade the beast for my TV and VCR. I threw in my food processor and microwave, and they paid my registration and taxes.

I drove the Nova out of the lot and went straight to Vinnie. I pulled into a parking space at the corner of Hamilton and Olden, extracted the key from the ignition, and waited for the car to thrash itself off. I said a short prayer not to be spotted by anyone I knew, wrenched the door open, and scuttled the short distance to the storefront office. The blue and white sign over the door read "Vincent Plum Bail Bonding Company." In smaller letters it advertised twenty-four-hour nationwide service. Conveniently located between Tender Loving Care Dry Cleaners and Fiorello's Deli, Vincent Plum catered to the family trade—domestic disturbances, disorderlies, auto theft, DWI, and shoplifting. The office was small and generic, consisting of two rooms with cheap walnut paneling on the walls and commercial grade rust-colored carpet on the floor. A Danish modern couch upholstered in brown Nauga-hyde pressed against one wall of the reception area, and a black and brown metal desk with a multiline phone and a computer terminal occupied a far corner.

Vinnie's secretary sat behind the desk, her head bent in concentration, picking her way through a stack of files. "Yeah?"

"I'm Stephanie Plum. I've come to see my cousin, Vinnie."

"Stephanie Plum!" Her head came up. "I'm Connie Rosolli. You went to school with my little sister, Tina. Oh jeez, I hope you don't have to make bail."

I recognized her now. She was an older version of Tina. Thicker in the waist, heavier in the face. She had lots of teased black hair, flawless olive skin, and a five-o'clock shadow on her upper lip.

"The only thing I have to make is money," I said to Connie. "I hear Vinnie needs someone to do filing."

"We just filled that job, and between you and me, you didn't miss anything. It was a crummy job. Paid minimum wage, and you had to spend all day on your knees singing the alphabet song. My feeling is, if you're going to spend that much time on your knees, you could find something that pays better. You know what I mean?"

"Last time I was on my knees was two years ago. I was looking for a contact lens."

"Listen, if you really need a job, why don't you get Vinnie to let you do skip tracing? There's good money in it."

"How much money?"

"Ten percent of the bond." Connie pulled a file from her top drawer. "We got this one in yesterday. Bail was set at $100,000, and he didn't show up for a court appearance. If you could find him and bring him in, you'd get $10,000."

I put a hand to the desk to steady myself. "Ten thousand dollars for finding one guy? What's the catch?"

"Sometimes they don't want to be found, and they shoot at you. But that hardly ever happens." Connie leafed through the file. "The guy who came in yesterday is local. Morty Beyers started tracking him down, so some of the prelim is already done. You've got pictures and everything."

"What happened to Morty Beyers?"

"Busted appendix. Happened at eleven-thirty last night. He's in St. Francis with a drain in his side and a tube up his nose."

I didn't want to wish Morty Beyers any misfortune, but I was starting to get excited about the prospect of stepping into his shoes. The money was tempting, and the job title had a certain cachet. On the other hand, catching fugitives sounded scary, and I was a certifiable coward when it came to risking my body parts.

"My guess is, it wouldn't be hard to find this guy," Connie said. "You could go talk to his mother. And if it gets hairy, you could back out. What have you got to lose?"

Only my life. "I don't know. I don't like the part about the shooting."

"Probably, it's like driving the turnpike," Connie said. "Probably, you get used to it. The way I see it, living in New Jersey is a challenge, what with the toxic waste and the eighteen-wheelers and the armed schizophrenics. I mean, what's one more lunatic shooting at you?"

Pretty much my own philosophy. And the $10,000 was damned appealing. I could pay off my creditors and straighten my life out. "Okay," I said. "I'll do it."

"You have to talk to Vinnie first." Connie swiveled her chair toward Vinnie's office door.

"Hey Vinnie!" she yelled. "You got business out here."

Vinnie was forty-five, 5' 7" without his lifts, and had the slim, boneless body of a ferret. He wore pointy-toed shoes, liked pointy-breasted women and dark-skinned young men, and he drove a Cadillac Seville.

"Steph here wants to do some skip tracing," Connie said to Vinnie.

"No way. Too dangerous," Vinnie said. "Most of my agents used to be in security. And you have to know something about law enforcement."

"I can learn about law enforcement," I told him.

"Learn about it first. Then come back."

"I need the job *now*."

"Not my problem."

I figured it was time to get tough. "I'll make it your problem, Vinnie. I'll have a long talk with Lucille."

Lucille was Vinnie's wife and the only woman in the Burg who didn't know about Vinnie's addiction to kinky sex. Lucille had her eyes firmly closed, and it wasn't my place to pry them open. Of course, if she ever *asked* . . . that'd be a whole other ball game.

"You'd blackmail me? Your own cousin?"

"These are desperate times."

He turned to Connie. "Give her a few civil cases. Stuff that involves telephone work."

"I want this one," I said, pointing to the file on Connie's desk. "I want the $10,000 one."

"Forget it. It's a murder. I should never have posted bail, but he was from the Burg, and I felt sorry for his mother. Trust me, you don't need this kind of trouble."

"I need the money, Vinnie. Give me a chance at bringing him in."

"When hell freezes over," Vinnie said. "I don't get this guy back, I'm in the hole for a hundred grand. I'm not sending an amateur after him."

Connie rolled her eyes at me. "You'd think it was out of his pocket. He's owned by an insurance company. It's no big deal."

"So give me a week, Vinnie," I said. "If I don't get him in a week, you can turn it over to someone else."

"I wouldn't give you a half hour."

I took a deep breath and leaned close to Vinnie, whispering in his ear. "I know about Madam Zaretski and her whips and chains. I know about the boys. And I know about the duck."

He didn't say anything. He just pressed his lips together until they turned white, and I knew I had him. Lucille would throw up if she knew what he did to the duck. Then she'd tell her father, Harry the Hammer, and Harry would cut off Vinnie's dick.

"Who am I looking for?" I asked Vinnie.

Vinnie handed me the file. "Joseph Morelli."

My heart flipped in my chest. I knew Morelli had been involved in a homicide. It had been big news in the Burg, and details of the shooting had been splashed across the front page of the Trenton *Times*. VICE COP KILLS UN-ARMED MAN. That had been over a month ago, and other, more important, issues (like the exact amount of the lottery) had replaced talk of Morelli. In the absence of more information, I'd assumed the shooting had been in the line of duty. I hadn't realized Morelli'd been charged with murder.

The reaction wasn't lost to Vinnie. "From the look on your face, I'd say you know him."

I nodded. "Sold him a cannoli when I was in high school."

Connie grunted. "Honey, half of all the women in New Jersey have sold him their can-noli."

AND YOU WON'T WANT TO MISS
STEPHANIE PLUM'S LATEST OUTING

TO THE NINES

AVAILABLE IN HARDCOVER
FROM ST. MARTIN'S PRESS

My NAME IS Stephanie Plum and I was born and raised in the Chambersburg section of Trenton, where the top male activities are scarfing pastries and pork rinds and growing love handles. The pastry and pork rind scarfing I've seen firsthand. The love handle growing happens over time. Thank God for small favors.

The first guy I saw up close and personal was Joe Morelli. Morelli put an end to my virgin status and showed me a body that was masculine perfection . . . smooth and muscular and sexy. Back then Morelli thought a long-term commitment was twenty minutes. I was one of thousands who got to admire Morelli's best parts as he pulled his pants up and headed for the door.

Morelli's been in and out of my life since then. He's currently in and he's improved with age, butt included.

So the sight of a naked ass isn't exactly new to me, but the one I was presently watching took the cake. Punky Balog had an ass like Winnie the Pooh . . . big and fat and furry. Sad to say, that was where the similarity ended because, unlike Pooh Bear, there was nothing endearing or cuddly about Punky Balog.

I knew about Punky's ass because I was in my new sunshine yellow Ford Escape, sitting across from Punky's dilapidated row house, and Punky had his huge Pooh butt plastered against his second-story window. My sometime partner, Lula, was riding shotgun for me and Lula and I were staring up at the butt in open-mouthed horror.

Punky slid his butt side to side on the pane and Lula and I gave a collective, upper lip curled back *eeyeuuw!*

"Think he knows we're out here," Lula said. "Think maybe he's trying to tell us something."

Lula and I work for my bail bonds agent cousin, Vincent Plum. Vinnie's office is on Hamilton Avenue, his big plate-glass front window looking into the Burg. He's not the world's best bonds agent. And he's not the worst. Truth is, he'd probably be a better bondsman if he wasn't saddled with Lula and me. I do fugitive apprehension for Vinnie and

I have a lot more luck than skill. Lula mostly does filing. Lula hasn't got luck or skill. The thing Lula has going for her is the ability to tolerate Vinnie. Lula's a plus-size black woman in a size-seven white world and Lula's had a lot of practice at pulling attitude.

Punky turned and gave us a wave with his johnson.

"That's just so sad," Lula said. "What do men think of? If you had a lumpy little wanger like that, would you go waving it in public?"

Punky was dancing now, jumping around, wanger flopping, doodles bouncing.

"Holy crap," Lula said. "He's gonna rupture something."

"It's gotta be uncomfortable."

"I'm glad we forgot the binoculars. I wouldn't want to see this up close."

I didn't even want to see it from a distance.

"When I was a ho I used to keep myself from getting grossed out by pretending men's privates were Muppets," Lula said. "This guy looks like an anteater Muppet. See the little tuft of hair on the anteater head and then there's the thing the anteater snuffs up ants with . . . except ol' Punky here's gotta get real close to the ants on account of his snuffer isn't real big. Punky's got a pinky."

Lula was a ho in a previous life. One night

while plying her trade she had a near-death experience and decided to change everything but her wardrobe. Not even a near-death experience could get Lula out of spandex. She was currently wearing a skintight hot pink miniskirt and a tiger-print top that made her boobs look like big round overinflated balloons. It was early June and midmorning and the Jersey air wasn't cooking yet, so Lula had a yellow angora sweater over the tiger top.

"Hold on," Lula said. "I think his snuffer is growing."

This produced another *eeyeuuw* from us.

"Maybe I should shoot him," Lula said.

"No shooting!" I felt the need to discourage Lula from hauling out her Glock, but truth was, it seemed like it'd be a public service to take a potshot at Punky.

"How bad do we want this guy?" Lula asked.

"If I don't bring him in, I don't get paid. If I don't get paid, I don't have rent money. If I don't have rent money, I get kicked out of my apartment and have to move in with my parents."

"So we want him real bad."

"*Real* bad."

"And he's wanted for what?"

"Grand theft auto."

"At least it's not armed robbery. I'm gonna be hoping the only weapon he's got, he's holding in his hand right now . . . on account of it don't look like much of a threat to me."

"I guess we should go do it."

"I'm ready to rock 'n' roll," Lula said. "I'm ready to kick some Punky butt. I'm ready to do the job."

I turned the key in the ignition. "I'm going to drop you at the corner so you can cut through the back and take the back door. Make sure you have your walkie-talkie on so I can let you know when I'm coming in."

"Roger, that."

"And no shooting, no breaking doors down, no Dirty Harry imitations."

"You can count on me."

Three minutes later, Lula reported she was in place. I parked the Escape two houses down, walked to Punky's front door, and rang the bell. No one responded so I rang a second time. I gave the door a solid rap with my fist and shouted, "Bond enforcement! Open the door!"

I heard shouting carrying over from the backyard, a door crashing open and slamming shut, and then more muffled shouting. I called Lula on the talkie, but got no response. A moment later the front door opened to the house next to me and Lula stomped out.

"Hey, so excuse me," she yelled at the woman behind her. "So I got the wrong door. It could happen, you know. We're under a lot of pressure when we're making these dangerous apprehensions."

The woman glared at Lula and slammed and locked her door shut.

"Must have miscounted houses," Lula said to me. "I sort of let myself in through the wrong door."

"You weren't supposed to open *any* door."

"Yeah, but I heard someone moving around inside. Guess that's 'cause it was the neighbor lady's house, hunh? So what's going on? How come you're not in yet?"

"He hasn't opened the door."

Lula took a step back and looked up. "That's because he's still mooning you."

I followed Lula's line of sight. She was right. Punky had his ass to the window again.

"Hey," Lula yelled up. "Get your fat ass off the window and get down here! We're trying to do some bond enforcement!"

An old man and an old woman came out of the house across the street and settled themselves on their front stoop to watch.

"Are you going to shoot him?" the old man wanted to know.

"I don't hardly ever get allowed to shoot anybody," Lula told him.

"That's darn disappointing," the man said. "How about kicking the door down?"

Lula gave the man one of her hand-on-hip *get real* looks. "Kick the door down? Do I look like I could kick a door down in these shoes? These are Via Spigas. You don't go around kicking down doors in Via Spigas. These are classy shoes. I paid a shitload of money for these shoes and I'm not sticking them through some cheap-ass door."

Everyone looked at me. I was wearing jeans, a T-shirt topped by a black jeans jacket, and CAT boots. CAT boots could definitely kick down a door, but they'd have to be on someone else's foot because door kicking was a skill I lacked.

"You girls need to watch more television," the old man said. "You need to be more like those Charlie's Angels. Nothing stopped them girls. They could kick doors down in all kinds of shoes."

"Anyways, you don't need to kick the door in," the old woman said. "Punky never locks it."

I tried the door and, sure enough, it was unlocked.

"Sort of takes the fun out of it," Lula said, looking past the door into Punky's house.

This is the part where if we were Charlie's

Angels we'd get into crouched positions, holding our guns in two hands in front of us, and we'd hunt down Punky. This didn't work for us because I left my gun home, in the cookie jar on my kitchen counter, and Lula'd fall over if she tried to do the crouch thing in her Via Spigas.

"Hey Punky," I yelled up the stairs, "put some clothes on and come down here. I need to talk to you."

"No way."

"If you don't get down here, I'm going to send Lula up to get you."

Lula's eyes got wide and she mouthed, *Me? Why me?*

"Come up here and get me," Punky said. "I have a surprise for you."

Lula pulled a Glock out of her handbag and gave it over to me. "You should take this on account of *you're* gonna be the one going up the stairs first and you might need it. You know how I hate surprises."

"I don't want the gun. I don't like guns."

"*Take* the *gun.*"

"I don't want the gun," I told her.

"*Take* the *gun!*"

Yeesh. "Okay, okay. Give me the stupid gun."

I got to the top of the stairs and I peeked around the corner, down the hall.

"Here I come, ready or not," Punky sang out. And then he jumped from behind a bedroom door and stood spread-eagle in full view. "Ta-dahhhh."

He was buck naked and slick as a greased pig. Lula and I swallowed hard and we both took a step backward.

"What have you got all over you?" I asked.

"Vaseline. Head to toe and extra heavy in the cracks and crevices." He was smiling ear to ear. "You want to take me in, you have to wrestle with me."

"How about we just shoot you," Lula said.

"You can't shoot me. I'm not armed."

"Here's the plan," I said to Lula. "We cuff him and put him in leg irons and then we wrap him in a blanket so he doesn't get my car greasy."

"I'm not touching him," Lula said. "Not only is he an ugly naked motherfucker, but he's a dry cleaning bill waiting to happen. I'm not ruining this top. I'll never find another top like this. It's genuine fake tiger. And Lord knows what he'd do to rabbit."

I reached for him with the cuffs. "Give me your hand."

"Make me," he said, waggling his butt. "Come get me, sweetie pie."

Lula looked over at me. "You *sure* you don't want me to shoot him?"

I took my jacket off and snatched at his wrist, but I couldn't hold tight. After three attempts I had Vaseline up to my elbow, and Punky was skipping around going, ". . . Nah, nah, nah. Kiss my can, you can't catch me, I'm the Vaseline man."

"This guy's in the red zone on the Breathalyzer," Lula said. "Think he might also be missing a few marbles in his greased-up jug head."

"I'm crazy like a fox," Punky said. "If you can't catch hold of me, you can't take me in. If you can't take me in, I don't go to jail."

"If I don't take you in, I don't pay my rent and I get kicked out of my apartment," I told Punky, lunging for him, swearing when he slid away from me.

"This here's embarrassing," Lula said. "I can't believe you're trying to grab this funky fat man."

"It's my job. And you could help! Take the damn top off if you don't want it to get ruined."

"Yeah, take your top off, momma. I've got plenty of extra Vaseline for you," Punky sang out.

Punky turned away from me, I gave him a good hard kick to the back of his knee, and he crashed to the floor. I threw myself on top of him and yelled to Lula to cuff him. She managed to get both cuffs on and my cell phone chirped.

It was my Grandma Mazur on the phone. When my Grandpa Mazur cashed in his two-dollar chips and moved on to the High Rollers' Suite in the sky, my Grandma Mazur moved in with my parents.

"Your mother's locked herself in the bathroom and she won't come out," Grandma said. "She's been in there for an hour and a half. It's the menopause. Your mother was always so sensible until the menopause hit."

"She's probably taking a bath."

"That's what I thought at first, but she's never in there this long. I went up and yelled and banged on the door just now and there's no answer. For all I know, she's dead. She could have had a heart attack and drowned in the tub."

"*Omigod.*"

"Anyways, I thought you could get over here and unlock the door like you did last time when your sister locked herself in the bathroom."

At Christmastime my sister Valerie locked herself in the bathroom with a pregnancy test kit. The test kit kept turning up positive, and if I was Valerie I would have wanted to spend the rest of my life locked in the bathroom, too.

"I wasn't the one who unlocked the door," I told Grandma. "I was the one who climbed onto the roof over the back stoop and went in through the window."

"Well, whatever you did, you better get over here and do it again. Your father's off somewhere and your sister's out. I'd shoot the lock off, but last time I tried to do that the bullet ricocheted off the doorknob and took out a table lamp."

"Are you sure this is an emergency? I'm sort of in the middle of something."

"Hard to tell what's an emergency in this house anymore."

My parents lived in a small three-bedroom, one-bathroom house that was bursting at the seams with my mom and dad, my grandma, my recently divorced, very pregnant sister, and her two kids. Emergencies tended to blend with the normal.

"Hang tight," I told Grandma. "I'm not far away. I'll be there in a couple minutes."

Lula looked down at Punky. "What are we gonna do with him?"

"We're going to take him with us."

"The hell you are," Punky said. "I'm not getting up. I'm not going anywhere."

"I don't have time to mess with this," I said

to Lula. "You stay here and baby-sit and I'll send Vinnie over to do the pickup."

"You're in trouble now," Lula said to Punky. "I bet Vinnie likes greased-up fat men. People tell me Vinnie used to be romantically involved with a duck. I bet he's gonna think you're just fine."

I hustled down the stairs and out the front door to the Escape. I called Vinnie on the way to my parents' house and gave him the word on Punky.

"What are you, nuts?" Vinnie yelled at me. "I'm not gonna go out to pick up some greased-up naked guy. I write bonds. I don't do pickups. Read my lips . . . *you're the pickup person.*"

"Fine. Then you go to my parents' house and get my mother out of the bathroom."

"All right, all right, I'll do your pickup, but it's come to a sad state of affairs when I'm the normal member of this family."

I couldn't argue with that one.

Grandma Mazur was waiting for me when I pulled to the curb. "She's still in there," Grandma said. "She won't talk to me or nothing."

I ran up the stairs and tried the door. Locked. I knocked. No answer. I yelled to my mother. Still no response. Damn. I ran down the stairs out to the garage and got a step ladder. I put the ladder up to the back stoop and climbed onto the small shingled roof that attached to the back of the house and gave me access to the bathroom window. I looked inside.

My mom was in the tub with earphones on, eyes closed, knees sticking out of the water like two smooth pink islands. I rapped on the window, and my mom opened her eyes and gave a shriek. She grabbed for the towel and continued to scream for a good sixty seconds. Finally she blinked, snapped her mouth shut, pointed straight-armed to the bathroom door, and mouthed the word *go*.

I scuttled off the roof, down the ladder, and slunk back to the house and up the stairs, followed by Grandma Mazur.

My mother was at the bathroom door, wrapped in a towel, waiting. "What the hell were you doing?" she yelled. "You scared the crap out of me. Dammit. Can't I even relax in the tub?"

Grandma Mazur and I were speechless, standing rooted to the spot, our mouths open, our eyes wide. My mom never cursed. My mom was the practical, calming influence on the family. My mom went to church. My mom *never* said *crap*.

"It's the change," Grandma said.

"It is *not* the change," my mother shouted. "I am not menopausal. I just want a half hour alone. Is that too much to ask? A crappy half hour!"

"You were in there for an hour and a half," Grandma said. "I thought you might have had a heart attack. You wouldn't answer me."

"I was listening to music. I didn't hear you. I had the headset on."

"I can see that now," Grandma said. "Maybe I should try that sometime."

My mother leaned forward and took a closer look at my shirt. "What on earth do you have all over you? It's in your hair and on your shirt and you have big grease stains on your jeans. It looks like . . . Vaseline."

"I was in the middle of a capture when Grandma called."

My mother did an eye roll. "I don't want to know the details. Not ever. And you should be sure to pretreat when you get home or you're never going to get that stuff out."

TEN MINUTES LATER I was pushing through the front door to Vinnie's office. Connie Rosolli, Vinnie's office manager and guard dog, was behind her desk, newspaper in hand. Connie was a couple years older than me, an inch or two shorter, and had me by three cup sizes. She was wearing a blood red V-neck sweater that showed a lot of cleavage. Her nails and her lips matched the sweater.

There were two women occupying the chairs in front of Connie's desk. Both women were dark-skinned and wearing traditional Indian dress. The older woman was a size up from Lula. Lula is packed solid, like a giant bratwurst. The woman sitting across from Connie was loose flab with rolls of fat cascading between the halter top and the long skirt of her sari. Her black hair was tied in a knot low on her neck and shot through with gray. The younger woman was slim and I guessed slightly younger than me. Late twenties, maybe. They both were perched on the edges of their seats, hands tightly clasped in their laps.

"We've got trouble," Connie said to me. "There's an article in the paper today about Vinnie."

"It's not another duck incident, is it?" I asked.

"It's about the visa bond Vinnie wrote for Samuel Singh. Singh is here on a three-month work visa and Vinnie wrote a bond insuring Singh would leave when his visa was up. A visa bond is a new thing, so the paper's making a big deal about it."

Connie handed me the paper and I looked at the photo accompanying the feature. Two slim, shifty-looking men with slicked-back black hair, smiling. Singh was from India, his complexion darker, his frame smaller than Vinnie's. Both men looked like they regularly conned old ladies out of their life savings. Two Indian women stood in the background, behind Vinnie and Singh. The women in the photo were the women sitting in front of Connie.

"This is Mrs. Apusenja and her daughter Nonnie," Connie said. "Mrs. Apusenja rented a room to Samuel Singh."

Mrs. Apusenja and her daughter were staring at me, not sure what to do or say about the globs of goo in my hair and gunked into my clothes.

"And this is Stephanie Plum," Connie told the Apusenjas. "She's one of our bond enforcement agents. She's not usually this . . . greasy." Connie squinted at me. "What the hell have you got all over you?"

"Vaseline. Balog was covered with it. I had to wrestle him down."

"This looks sexual to me," Mrs. Apusenja said. "I am a moral woman. I do not want to become involved with this." She clapped her hands to her head. "Look at me. I have my ears covered. I am not hearing this filth."

"There's no filth," I shouted at her. "There was this guy I had to bring in and he was covered in Vaseline . . ."

"Lalalalalalala," Mrs. Apusenja sang.

Connie and I rolled our eyes.

Nonnie pulled her mother's hand away from her head. "Listen to these people," she said to her mother. "We need them to help us."

Mrs. Apusenja stopped singing and crossed her arms over her chest.

"Mrs. Apusenja is here because Singh's disappeared," Connie said.

"This is true," Mrs. Apusenja said. "We are very worried. He was an exemplary young man."

I skimmed the article. Samuel Singh's bond was up in a week. If Vinnie couldn't produce Singh in a week's time, he was going to look like an idiot.

"We think something terrible happened to him," Nonnie said. "He just disappeared. *Poof.*"

The mother nodded in agreement. "Samuel has been staying with us while working in this country. My family is very close to Samuel Singh's family in India. It's a very good family.

Nonnie and Samuel were to be married, in fact. She was to travel to India with Samuel to meet his mother and father. We have a ticket for the plane."

"How long has Samuel been gone?" Connie asked.

"Five days," Nonnie said. "He left for work and he never returned. We asked his employer and they said Samuel didn't show up that day. We came here because we hoped Mr. Plum would be able to help us find Samuel."

"Have you checked Samuel's room to see if anything is missing?" I asked. "Clothes? Passport?"

"Everything seems to be there."

"Have you reported his disappearance to the police?"

"We have not. Do you think we should do that?"

"No," Connie said, voice just a tad too shrill, hitting Vinnie's cell phone number on her speed dial.

"We've got a situation here," Connie said to Vinnie. "Mrs. Apusenja is in the office. Samuel Singh has gone missing."

AT TWO IN the morning when the weather is ideal and the lights are all perfectly timed, it takes twenty minutes to drive from the police station to the bail bonds office. Today, at two in the afternoon, under an overcast sky, Vinnie made the run in twelve minutes.

Ranger, Vinnie's top gun, had ambled in a couple minutes earlier at Vinnie's request. He was dressed in his usual black. His dark brown hair was pulled back from his face and tied into a short ponytail at the nape of his neck. His jacket looked suspiciously like Kevlar and I knew from experience it hid a gun. Ranger was always armed. And Ranger was always dangerous. His age was somewhere between twenty-five and thirty-five and his skin was the color of a mocha latte. The story goes that Ranger had been Special Forces before signing on with Vinnie to do bond enforcement. He had a lot of muscle and a skill level somewhere between Batman and Rambo.

A while ago Ranger and I spent the night together. We were in an uneasy alliance now, working as a team when necessary, avoiding contact or conversation that would lead to a repeat sexual encounter. At least I was avoiding a repeat encounter. Ranger was his usual silent mysterious self, his thoughts unknown, his attitude provocative.

He'd looked me over before taking a chair. "Vaseline?" he asked.

"I am thinking it must be something sexual," Mrs. Apusenja said. "No one has told me otherwise. I am thinking this one must be a slut."

"I am *not* a slut," I said. "I had to capture a guy who was all greased up and some of the gunk rubbed off on me."

The back door burst open and Vinnie came in like gangbusters, followed by Lula.

"Talk to me," Vinnie said to Connie.

"Not much to tell. You remember Mrs. Apusenja and her daughter Nonnie. Samuel Singh rented a room in the Apusenja house and they were at the photo session last week. They haven't seen him in five days."

"Christ," Vinnie said. "National print coverage on this. A week to go. And this sonovabitch goes missing. Why didn't he just come over to my house and feed me rat poison? It would have been an easier death."

"We think there might be foul play involved," Nonnie said.

Vinnie made a halfhearted effort to squash a grimace. "Yeah, right. Give me a refresher course on Samuel Singh. What was his normal routine?" Vinnie had the file in his hand, flipping pages, mumbling as he read. "It says here he worked at TriBro Tech. He was in the quality control department."

"During the week Samuel would be at work

from seven-thirty to five. Every night he would stay home and watch television or spend time on his computer. Even on weekends he would spend most of his time on the computer," Nonnie said.

"There is a word to call him," Mrs. Apusenja said. "I can never remember."

"Geek," Nonnie said, not looking all that happy about it.

"Yes! That's it. He was a computer geek."

"Did he have friends? Relatives in the area?" Vinnie asked.

"There were people at his workplace that he spoke of but he didn't spend time with them socially."

"Did he have enemies? Debts?"

Nonnie shook her head no. "He never spoke of debts or enemies."

"Drugs?" Vinnie asked.

"No. And he would drink alcohol only on special occasions."

"How about criminal activity? Was he involved with anyone shady?"

"Certainly not."

Ranger was impassive in his corner, watching the women. Nonnie was leaning forward in her chair, uncomfortable with the situation. Mama Apusenja had her lips pressed tight together, her head tipped slightly, not favorably impressed with what she was seeing.

"Anything else?" Vinnie asked.

Nonnie fidgeted in her seat. Her eyes dropped to the purse in her lap. "My little dog," Nonnie finally said. "My little dog is missing." She opened her purse and extracted a photo. "His name is Boo because he is so white. Like a ghost. He disappeared when Samuel vanished. He was in the backyard, which is fenced, and he disappeared."

We all looked at the photo of Nonnie and Boo. Boo was a small cocker spaniel and poodle mix with black button eyes in a fluffy white face. Boo was a cockapoo.

I felt something tug inside me for the dog. The black button eyes reminded me of my hamster, Rex. I remembered the times when I'd been worried about Rex, and I felt the same sharp stab of concern for the little dog.

"Do you get along okay with your neighbors?" Vinnie asked. "Have you asked any of them if they've seen the dog?"

"No one has seen Boo."

"We must leave now," Mrs. Apusenja said, glancing at her watch. "Nonnie needs to get back to work."

Vinnie saw them to the door and watched them cross the street to their car. "There they go," Vinnie said. "Hell's message bearers." He shook his head. "I was having such a good day. Everyone was saying how good I looked in the picture. Everyone was congratulating me because I was doing something about visa enforcement. Okay, so I took a few comments when I dragged a naked, greased-up fat guy into the station, but I could handle that." He gave his head another shake. "*This* I can't handle. This has to get fixed. I can't afford to lose this guy. Either we find this guy, dead or alive, or we're all unemployed. If I can't enforce this visa bond after all the publicity, I'm going to have to change my name, move to Scottsdale, Arizona, and sell used cars." Vinnie focused on Ranger. "You can find him, right?"

The corners of Ranger's mouth tipped up a fraction of an inch. This was the Ranger equivalent of a smile.

"I'm gonna take that as a yes," Vinnie said.

"I'll need help," Ranger told him. "And we'll need to work out the fee."

"Fine. Whatever. You can have Stephanie."

Ranger cut his eyes to me and the smile widened ever so slightly—the sort of smile you see on a man when he's presented with an unexpected piece of pie.

The "Plumography"— your guide to the world of all things Plum!

"There are some men who enter a woman's life and screw it up forever. Joseph Morelli did this to me—not forever, but periodically."

ONE FOR THE MONEY

Meet Stephanie Plum. The Trenton native just got laid off as discount lingerie buyer for E.E. Martin's in Newark, but the worst part is, she lost her cherished Mazda Miata to the repo man. Replacement: a used Nova with a bad muffler. A visit to her parents and her Grandma Mazur, who lives with them, leads to a light at the end of the Jersey Tunnel: a job with her cousin Vinnie at Vincent Plum Bail Bonding Company. Ten thousand a pop for hauling in the bad guys—guys like Joe Morelli, Stephanie's childhood nemesis-turned-hunky-vice-cop now wanted on a murder rap. Still as sexy and dangerous as ever, the heat is on—and working with just-as-hot fellow bondsman and mentor, Ranger, Stephanie could get burned. The bright side? Stephanie's junked her Nova and hijacked Morelli's Jeep Cherokee. Unfortunately, it's soon blown to smithereens. Packing pepper spray and a .38 Special, and with two new men in her life, it looks like a promising new career for Stephanie Plum . . .

1) Historic Moment: First book in the series.
2) New Characters Introduced: Stephanie Plum, Grandma Mazur, Cousin Vinnie, Joe Morelli, Ranger, Lula
3) Automotive Factoid: Stephanie drives a Nova and Jeep Cherokee.

"Morelli and I had done battle before. With only short-lived victories on both sides, I suspected this would be another war of sorts. And I figured I'd have to learn to live with it."

TWO FOR THE DOUGH

Stephanie Plum is trying to ease into her new job with a level head. It appears Joe Morelli is around for good—and bad—and she's resigned to it. Her loose professional relationship with Ranger ends in a platonic night together with no strings attached, and her new set of wheels, a secondhand Jeep Wrangler, suits her needs. Until it's stolen out from under her. How is she supposed to nab Kenny Mancuso, her new bail jumper and a distant relative of Morelli's? In a burst of misguided good intentions, she's strong-armed into accepting as a gift a 1953 Buick passed down from Grandma Mazur's brother, Sandor. It may look like a beluga whale but it's a car built to last—much to Stephanie's chagrin. Meanwhile, Morelli, whose libido has been stuck on overdrive ever since he met Stephanie years ago, is ready to make the moves on the resistant bounty hunter. Will she cave? Not on her Grandma's life—which happens to be in danger from an ice pick–wielding goon . . .

1) Historic Moment: Morelli's intentions become known, and the battle of the sexes begins.
2) New Characters Introduced: Kenny Mancuso, Eddie Gazarra, Mary Lou Stankovic
3) Automotive Factoid: Stephanie drives a Jeep Wrangler and a '53 Buick.

"I wasn't sure why I was still working for Vinnie. I suspected it had something to do with the title. Bounty hunter. It held a certain cachet. Even better, the job didn't require panty hose."

THREE TO GET DEADLY

Uncle Mo Bedemier may have a reputation as a kindly old candy-store owner but all that changes when he skips bail on a very minor charge. Bounty hunter Stephanie Plum needs to know why and that means scouting Uncle Mo's neighborhood. And no one knows Stark Street better than the new file clerk, Lula, a former hooker with an attitude—and better yet, a Nissan in working order. This seamier side of Jersey is where Stephanie comes to after a knock on the head, a corpse at her heels, and Joe Morelli on her tail as the possible murderer. Before the investigation is over, Ranger loses his Beemer, no thanks to Stephanie; the Nissan ends up in the shop for repairs; and Stephanie winds up with a green Mazda as loaner and red highlights in her hair. It certainly gets Morelli's attention because it prompts a first kiss on the back of Stephanie's very vulnerable neck . . .

1) Historic Moment: Morelli finally kisses Stephanie—and she's all for it.
2) New Characters Introduced: Uncle Moses Bedemier, Joyce Barnhardt, Stuart Baggett
3) Automotive Factoid: Stephanie drives a Nissan, a Mazda, and a '53 Buick.

> *"From here on out, Morelli was
> erotica non grata. 'Look but Don't Touch,'
> that was my motto."*

FOUR TO SCORE

It's been months since Joe Morelli made his move on Stephanie Plum, and true to form, it's been months since she's heard from him again. But the minute he returns, the rugged vice cop again proves irresistible—for at least one more night. She'd kick herself for giving in if she wasn't so preoccupied with a bail jumper: a waitress on the run for stealing her boyfriend's car. To make matters even worse, Vinnie's hired Joyce Barnhardt, Stephanie's high school rival and eventual home-wrecker, to join the bounty-hunting team as a skip tracer. Now, with the help of Lula riding shotgun in Stephanie's new Honda CRX, and a transvestite named Sally Sweet, Stephanie becomes embroiled in a game of murder, extortion, and kidnapping. Where it all leads is back into Morelli's arms—wrapped up on a motorcycle powered with 109 horses taking her to places she'd promised she'd never go again.

1) Historic Moment: Stephanie and Morelli "do the deed."

2) New Characters Introduced: Sally Sweet, Edward Kuntz
3) Automotive Factoid: Stephanie drives a Honda CRX and a '53 Buick.

"When I was a little girl I used to dress Barbie up without underpants . . . And being a bail enforcement agent is sort of like being a bare-bottom Barbie. It's about having a secret."

HIGH FIVE

With her Honda CRX now just a memory of blown-up cinders, Stephanie's back in her '53 Buick—a "classic," she defends. With *no* authority. But with absolute conviction she's on the hunt for a vanishing relative. According to Grandma Mazur, Uncle Fred's gone missing. Seventy years old, just left the bank, and an easy mark. It doesn't look good. Whatever link the disappearance has to the rough beating of her friend, Lula, Stephanie's determined to find it. By way of a Porsche, garbage truck, and a BMW, past a nasty, vertically-challenged bookie and a stun-gun-toting Grandma Mazur, and through a Mafia wedding, Stephanie's bound and determined to make it out alive. But whether she ends up with Ranger or Morelli—both of whom make their intentions known—is a fate that she leaves to the heavens . . . and a simple draw of the name.

1) Historic Moment: Stephanie gets the hots for Ranger.
2) New Characters Introduced: Uncle Fred, Aunt Mabel, Randy Briggs
3) Automotive Factoid: Stephanie drives a Porsche, a BMW, and a '53 Buick.

"Two of the men on my list of desirables actually desire me back. The problem being that they both sort of scare the hell out of me."

HOT SIX

Stephanie Plum's career as a bounty hunter may finally be taking its toll—on both her used Honda Civic and her emotions. Ranger has just been arrested by a rookie cop on a concealed weapons charge. Simple enough, until Ranger disappears. It seems he's also wanted in connection with the murder of a gun-trader's son. Now Stephanie wants Ranger in the worst way while Joe Morelli wants Stephanie in the *best* way. But Joe's private time is cramped by Grandma Mazur, who moves in with Stephanie for the forseeable future. That's not the only surprise Grandma has: a suitor, Eddie DeChooch, hints at an exquisite night of sin. Stephanie's not so lucky. After her car is torched, she ends up with a one-of-a-kind Rollswagon that's drawing stares, and a sideline as a dog-sitter. But her biggest concern—next to finding Ranger—is Grandma Mazur's bid for a driver's license. With the streets endangered and Stephanie's life turned upside down, Morelli offers what he can to help. To Stephanie's surprise it's a proposal of marriage . . .

1) Historic Moment: Grandma Mazur moves in with Stephanie, Morelli proposes, and Ranger's secret past is alluded to.
2) New Character Introduced: Eddie De-Chooch
3) Automotive Factoid: Stephanie drives a Honda Civic and a custom-built "Rollswagon" (and a '53 Buick).

"Morelli's still trouble . . . but now he's the kind of trouble a woman likes."

SEVEN UP

Joe Morelli? Marriage? Sharing a bathroom? He must be desperate. But is Stephanie? At least, desperate to put her new bounty hunt to rest, anyway. After getting caught smuggling a truckload of bootleg cigarettes up from Virginia, Eddie DeChooch missed his court date. Stephanie doesn't want to have anything to do with it. After all, Eddie not only left behind a bullet-riddled corpse in his garden, but he's dating her Grandma Mazur. It's all hitting a little too close to home—so does the bombshell news leveled by Stephanie's sister, Valerie: a marriage break-up that's brought the depressed wife back to her roots. While Stephanie's considering her own marriage to Morelli, two of her childhood friends vanish. For answers she turns to the only man who can help. Ranger's deal? He'll give Stephanie everything she needs—if she gives him everything he wants. Trouble is, what he wants, Stephanie wants just as bad! With divided attention between the two men in her life, Stephanie finally relents, and grants Ranger his wish, leaving Morelli behind. How big a mistake could it be? She's about to find out . . .

1) Historic Moment: Stephanie's sister Valerie moves in with the Plum family after her marriage fails.
2) New Characters Introduced: Valerie, Mooner, Ziggy and Benny
3) Automotive Factoid: Stephanie drives a Harley (and a '53 Buick).

*"A few months ago Ranger and I made a deal
that has haunted me—another one of those
jumping off the garage roof things, except this
deal involved my bedroom . . ."*

HARD EIGHT

Stephanie Plum is on the hunt for a mother
and child on the run who have left behind an
angry ex-husband. He's eager to collect on a
child custody bond. When local thug and busi-
nessman Eddie Abruzzi warns Stephanie to lay
off of the case, she's only more intrigued. And
a little scared, especially when she finds a bag
of snakes on her doorknob and tarantulas in
her car. What Stephanie needs is back-up, and
Ranger's more than available—for the bounty
hunt, and for Stephanie. Soon, a stalker in a
bunny suit is on Stephanie's tail, her CRV is
blown to bits, and a corpse winds up on her
couch. That's just one body too many in Stephanie's house, considering her Grandma Mazur
and sister, Valerie, have moved in, leaving little room for Joe Morelli, who wants back into
Stephanie's life. Before the case closes, she's
sure to find her man. It's the other two men
Stephanie has to contend with that are putting

the perplexed and love-sick bounty hunter's heart at risk . . .

1) Historic Moment: Stephanie knows that she must decide on her future with Morelli once and for all.
2) New Characters Introduced: Eddie Abruzzo, Mrs. Markowitz, Carol Nadich, Evelyn Soder, Albert Kloughn
3) Automotive Factoid: Stephanie drives a Honda CR-V (not to mention a '53 Buick).